George P. Fisher

Out of the Woods

A Romance of Camp Life

George P. Fisher

Out of the Woods
A Romance of Camp Life

ISBN/EAN: 9783744641265

Printed in Europe, USA, Canada, Australia, Japan

Cover: Foto ©Andreas Hilbeck / pixelio.de

More available books at **www.hansebooks.com**

OUT OF THE WOODS

A ROMANCE OF CAMP LIFE

BY

GEORGE P. FISHER, Jr.

CHICAGO

A. C. McCLURG AND COMPANY

1896

THIS LITTLE BOOK IS DEDICATED TO THOSE IN WHOSE

GENIAL FELLOWSHIP

I LEARNED TO LOVE THE WOODS.

G. P. F., JR.

CHICAGO, JUNE, 1896.

OUT OF THE WOODS.

CHAPTER I.

ROBERT FERRIS lounged on the window-seat of his quarters at the C—— Club finishing his after-dinner cigar, and watched the moon as it rose over Lake Michigan, giving a touch of picturesqueness to Chicago's most unattractive harbor. He was perplexed, and the cause lay in the telegram and the letter which he held in his hand. The telegram, which was from the manager of the Gloria mine, stated that the feeling among the strikers was hourly growing more serious, and urged him to come at once. The letter was from his oldest friend, Captain Philip Vinton, a retired naval officer, saying that on the next day he would reach Chicago, where he was to join a party of friends for a month's outing in the woods of northern Michigan.

Ferris's father, Edward Ferris, also a naval officer, had been killed in the early part of our civil war by the bursting of a cannon. The same

7

accident had nearly cost Vinton his life, and had so affected his eyesight that when peace came and he wanted to enjoy the ample fortune that he had inherited, he found no difficulty in getting retired from active service, while he devoted himself more actively to his pet philanthropic scheme — the Sailor's Rest at Lynn.

Edward Ferris and Philip Vinton, in childhood, had been like devoted brothers. They had dreamed of the sea together, and had sailed their toy boats in many a hotly contested regatta on the fish pond of the Vinton homestead at the foot of the Kaaterskills. Together they had hunted for the hidden treasures of Captain Kidd and Hendrik Hudson, sharing in their long tramps over the mountains the glory and burden of a time-honored fowling-piece, with which they vainly hoped to encounter the twelve-tined buck that some seasons before had been reported as seen thereabouts. Later they had gone to the Naval Academy, and, happily for them, made together the long cruise at the end of their course. Upon their return each received promotion, and then came their first long separation, Vinton being sent to the South Atlantic Squadron and Ferris being assigned to shore duty at Newport. There Ferris married, and for two years was the happiest of men; but his young wife died when their little boy, Robert,

was less then a year old, and then, at Vinton's
urgent solicitation, he joined him on the " Macedonian " as it was ordered to sail for Lisbon in
the fall of 1860. Vinton's happy companionship
was a God-send to poor Ferris, and served, as
nothing else could have done, to lift him from
the despondency into which he had sunk after
his wife's death.

Robert Ferris inherited from his father this
man's devoted friendship, and upon the death of
his grandmother while he was preparing for college, made Vinton's house his home. As he had
elected to take the scientific course, with mining
engineering as a specialty, his summer vacations
were spent chiefly in the mountains of Montana
and Colorado, and the fine heads of elk and
deer that adorned the hallway of the club and
the dining-room of Vinton's home were ample
proof that his vacations had not been devoid of
sport. Indeed, it needed but a glance at the
hunting and fishing paraphernalia, which he
periodically rummaged over, to show that he was
a lover of the woods. This was another bond of
union between Ferris and Vinton, for the latter,
although a wretched rifle shot, was fond of
shooting and was a devoted angler. Next to
going on a hunting trip with "Uncle Phil," as
Ferris had always called Vinton, there was
nothing that he enjoyed more than talking over

past excursions and planning new ones with him. And so it was that Ferris reached his decision to take the midnight train for Keating, near which the Gloria mine was located, with a double feeling of regret that he would miss meeting his dearest friend, whom he had not seen for nearly six months, and would lose the chance of talking over the prospective camping trip, and of selecting with him from his own abundant store of such things the choicest rifle and the best assortment of trout flies, rods and tackle.

When Ferris had decided that he could not delay his departure until Vinton came, he busied himself with packing, and then began collecting such things as he thought Vinton might need for his outing. While thus occupied there was a knock at his door.

"Come in, Tom;" he called from his store-room, recognizing the familiar rap, and as Tom Moulton opened the door he added; "You are the very man I wanted to see."

Tom Moulton, as he was familiarly known to all club-men, was a handsome fellow, six feet tall, with a frankness of voice and manner and an endless fund of good fellowship that made him the most popular man of his set.

"I thought you might care to see me, Bob;" he said, as he closed the door after him; "and

at great sacrifice of my valuable time I have
come up here.   In an evil moment I picked up
the 'Evening Journal' in the reading-room, and
my eye caught these headlines : 'The great
strike at the Gloria mine !' 'Locked-out miners
threatening to destroy the shaft,' etc., etc.   I
said to myself, 'That means that Bob Ferris will
go north to-night and will need the benefit of
my valuable advice as to the best method of
quelling a labor riot, and incidentally my assistance in getting his affairs in shape for the
journey.'   So I have let the Thomas concert go,
and here I am, ready to make a martyr of myself. Give me a cigar and tell me where to begin."

"Help yourself to a cigar, and sit down while
I tell you how you really can be of assistance. I
have just had a letter from Uncle Phil Vinton,
saying that he will be here in the morning *en
route* to northern Michigan where he is to take
a month's shooting and fishing. The dear old
fellow will probably bring an ancient Springfield
rifle, a muzzle-loading shot-gun and a dilapidated fishing rod, all resurrected from the
trumpery of his attic, and a book of moth-eaten
flies, if he remembers to bring any, which I
doubt. You know that when he gets anything
of the kind worth keeping he invariably sends it
to me. Now I want you to give him these
things I have laid out. Don't let him examine

the Winchester too closely, for if he sees that the calibre is only forty, he will scorn it as a pop-gun, whereas it is large enough for anything smaller than a grizzly. Insist upon his taking this rod, and if he thinks it too light, you may invent some convincing fiction, such as my having landed a tarpon with it on the gulf coast last fall. There is no one so obstinate as an old fisherman, and when he becomes attached to a rod he is apt to consider it suitable for any fish that swims."

"Can I use the same tarpon story in commending the flies? I don't wish to tax my imagination too severely."

"Well, hardly. You need only show him his own, which he has probably not seen since the moths began their depredations. You must see, too, that he takes this leather vest and brown sweater, for the nights will be cold, and he is as improvident as the cricket of the fable. After he has agreed to take all of these, you can show him the rest of the stuff in my store-room and see that he has everything he may need."

"Don't you think that you had better provide an old lady to go along and see that he is properly wrapped up before he exposes himself to the night air, and that the warming-pan is heated to the right temperature before he goes to bed?"

"No, stupid. There are to be several women in his party, I understand, and I will trust them to look after the domestic arrangements."

"Are they young or old, Bob?"

"I thought that would arouse your interest. His letter says there are to be two young ladies and a chaperon, and two men besides himself."

"Do you think they would like an extra man —myself, for instance? You know I have never seen a deer outside the Zoo, and you have often urged me to try an outing in the woods."

"You might ask him when he comes. Frankly, I think such a party would please you well, for I am sorry to say, you have not the first instincts of a hunter. But the trip would give you a taste of the woods without depriving you of that essential to your existence—female society. You could entertain the women while the other fellows get the sport."

"Well, I like that. Can't you imagine a camping trip pleasant if there happen to be a girl in the party?"

"Yes, but I must imagine the girl, also, Tom, for I have never seen her."

"You will though some day, and when the time comes, look out. For your sake, old man, I trust that when you do find your Diana she will recognize in you one worthy to follow her hounds."

"Thanks, Tom, but I shall not look for her —at least not just now. Some day I trust I may meet some honest girl, sound in body, mind and heart, having tastes with which mine will harmonize, and then —"

"And then, you think that you will take the matter under advisement, weigh the evidence carefully, as our lawyers say, and on bended knee offer your deliberate affirmative decision. Now, my dear fellow, you will do nothing of the kind. To a man of your honesty and fine feeling matrimony doesn't come that way. If it comes to you at all — which I doubt, for you see so little of women, and there is everything in propinquity — it will be a chance, and a happy one I hope. Some men marry for companionship, but they are not of your temperament or tastes. I might do such a thing when I grow old and cease to interest the general feminine public."

"That time will never come, Tom, or if it does you will never recognize it. Don't you want to ride over to the station with me ?" he added, looking at his watch. "My train starts in half an hour."

"Yes, and I can then catch the last half of the concert."

On the way to the station, Ferris gave Moulton an outline of his plan for settling the difficulties at the mines. Not that he questioned whether it would meet his approval, but he knew it would interest him.

As they walked down the platform, Moulton, with his arm on Ferris's shoulder and with genuine anxiety in his tone, begged him not to rely too much upon the fairness of his men.

"I had the misfortune," he said, "to be a lieutenant in the New York Seventh during a labor riot. Until then I was a great believer in arbitration ; but I learned, at the cost of numerous bruises, that it is foolish to attempt arbitration with a mob until you have first thrashed it or at least have convinced it of your power to do so. Don't take any chances, Bob, for if the men believe that they have been wronged by your company, they will be slow to recognize that you, an officer of the company, are working in their interest. It would be poor comfort to your friends to know that you had played the rôle of martyr."

The train started, and as Moulton watched it draw out of the station he wished that he had accompanied Ferris on this journey, which he felt might be attended with danger.

After leaving Ferris at the station, Moulton drove to the Thomas concert, arriving there just before the last intermission. There was a retired corner under one of the galleries in the old Exposition building, in which the concerts were then held, well known to a few music lovers, and to this he was hurrying around the edge of the audience when he saw coming towards him his old class-mate, Merrick Whitney, accompanied by a tall, raw-boned and weather-beaten young man who was unmistakably English or Scotch. Moulton had seen but little of Whitney for several years, as the latter, after leaving college, had spent four years abroad studying chemistry, and on his return to this country had buried himself in a New York laboratory in the study of bacteriology until his health became impaired, since which time he had been looking after his father's ranch in Wyoming.

Whitney's face beamed as he saw Moulton, for they had been close friends in college, and grasping his hands he drew him behind some potted palms and evergreens away from the audience. The Scotchman, for such he was, followed at a little distance and joined them as Whitney was making Moulton promise to meet them at the club after the concert.

"I want you to meet my friend, Blake-Kennedy," he said, as the latter came up, and added: "Kennedy, this is my old friend, Tom Moulton, of whom you have heard Helen speak, no doubt. Moulton has just promised to join us

at the club later and we will show him a ranch-
man's idea of a late supper. By the way, Tom,
do you know Helen is here? You will find
her with mother in that dismal corner under
the left gallery near the stage. You had better
not go near her unless you are in tune; she has
just sent us off because she said that we were
out of tune and spoiled the music for her."

As Moulton approached the corner he saw
Mrs. Whitney leaning languidly against one of
the pillars next to which she was sitting and
evidently more interested in watching her
daughter than in listening to the music. He
stopped at a little distance and watched Helen
too. She was bending forward with her hands
clasped in front of her, eagerly drinking in the
music of the 'cello-obligato and altogether unmindful of the world about her. When the
solo was finished and the orchestra took up the
theme, a faint smile passed over her face and,
drawing a long, quivering breath, she leaned
back again in her chair, listening now with half-
closed eyes until the premature applause broke
the spell, then passing her hand across her face
she turned and saw Moulton coming toward
her. There was genuine pleasure in her face as
she greeted him.

"This is indeed delightful," said she, "and
how strange that we should meet on the very

spot where we said good-bye nearly a year ago. I looked for you when we came in, for you care for music, while Merrick and Mr. Kennedy do not, and mamma does not hear well enough to get much pleasure from it. I concluded that if you were here your friend, Mr. Ferris, had hidden you in some spot where his enjoyment would not be disturbed by the sight of woman. Does he shun women as persistently as ever?"

"Woman in the concrete, yes," answered Moulton, with a laugh, "but for woman in the abstract he still remains, as our diplomatists say, 'with renewed assurance of profoundest consideration.'"

"Which, in his case, as in diplomacy, means nothing. Where is he now?"

"On his way to Keating. You know — or perhaps you have not noticed — there are serious labor troubles at the Gloria mine, and Ferris was telegraphed for to-day."

"Then it is possible that we may meet him. Did Merrick tell you that we start to-morrow night for an outing in Northern Michigan? I think our camp will be not far from Keating. Then, too, we shall have Captain Vinton with us, and if we are accessible at all, Mr. Ferris will have to come and see his uncle, even at the risk of meeting a woman. Don't you think you had better write or telegraph and warn him?"

"Now, really, you do not understand Ferris. He is not a woman-hater. He admires, yes, and absurd as it sounds, enjoys women as much as any man I know, but though apparently self-possessed in their presence, he is really ill at ease. The few times I have induced him to call with me have proven not only that he heartily enjoys their society but that he has a rare faculty of making himself entertaining and attractive to them."

"That is the most exasperating feature of his case. If he were stupid we could pardon his indifference; or if he were a genius and uninteresting, as geniuses so often are, his utter disregard would give us no concern; but unfortunately he is neither. I feel that I am on most intimate terms with your friend, for you have brought him to see me twice, which is double the attention he has shown any other girl. But tell me now, what have you been doing in music since I saw you last?"

"I have been a trifler, as ever. I have done but little singing, because I have not the perseverance to practice scales and breathing and syllables in the way that is essential to success, and I am tired of being told, as a supposed compliment, that I really ought to study. You will smile when I tell you that I have been struggling with the banjo at the rate of four lessons a week for the past six months, and am getting so that I can play fairly well."

"There is something incongruous about a banjo accompaniment to your voice, but I do not despise the banjo by any means, for it has a weirdness and individuality, and in the open air especially I like it. Can you imagine a more appropriate instrument to be played at a camp fire in the heart of the forest on an autumn night? I wish you were going with us."

"On behalf of my banjo, thanks. Who are to be in your party?"

"Well, first in order of importance is Mrs. Elting."

"She is the cook, I suppose."

"No, this is not to be exclusively a man's party. Mrs. Elting is the chaperon and a most delightful little woman. Her husband owns the lumber mill and the little town about it from which our expedition starts, and in the winter they live in Detroit. Then there is Miss Seaton, who is really the Major-General of the expedition, as she organized it and with the aid of dear old Colonel Elting, who has furnished everything in the way of camp-outfit, has looked after all the details. The men of the party are Captain Vinton, Mr. Kennedy and Merrick. Have you ever been camping?"

"Never, and yet I am so fond of the country

that I cannot imagine a more delightful way of spending a vacation with an agreeable party."

"I am sure our party must prove congenial. Miss Seaton and I have been together constantly during the past year. We roomed together in Berlin last fall and winter. She spent July with us at Nantucket, and I have just come from visiting her in Detroit. She is with us now, but preferred to spend this last evening in civilization looking after our supply lists and seeing that we have everything necessary in the way of rods and guns and ammunition."

"She must be a veritable modern Diana," said Moulton with a smile.

"She is the most fascinating girl I have ever known. She is not exactly what would be called beautiful, from a woman's point of view, although if she dressed more conventionally this might be different. Her face is dark and her features, although small, have an almost masculine precision. Do you recall Gerault's picture of the 'Shepherdess?' If so, you will recognize the resemblance, when you see Miss Seaton. She has done a great deal of hunting and fishing, and her home has many trophies to attest her skill both with shot-gun and rifle. Ever since she was a child and until two years ago she has spent several months of each year in the woods where we are to camp. She lives with her uncle,

Dr. Burton, and her aunt, Miss Burton, who is quite old and a confirmed invalid. She is very different from any girl I ever knew, and although a great student, particularly in chemistry and history, she is most enthusiastic about out-of-door life and sports."

"Her masculine traits evidently attract you."

"Yet withal, she is so entirely womanly. Her room struck me, I remember, as so thoroughly characteristic of herself. The brass bed with its soft white canopy, the exquisite daintiness of the white and gilt furniture, showing the most delicate womanly taste, while over the mantel were the antlers of a great buck, and beneath these a bamboo rod and a rifle. The fire-screen was the skin of a loon she had shot, beautifully mounted with outspread wings in a brass frame, and upon the hearth was a great black bear skin with head and claws complete, which she says her uncle assures her that she shot, although she protests that she was too much frightened to remember having done so. But you must come over to-morrow and dine with our party, for we do not start until 9 o'clock. Perhaps if you exert yourself you can so impress Miss Seaton that she will invite you to join us in the woods. That would be delightful. Don't you really think you would enjoy it?"

"Yes, I am sure I should. I have never been

camping but I have always loved the woods, and I remember how, as a small boy, when we lived in the country near Leamington — you recall the dear place — my favorite way of spending a holiday was to get my chum, Tom Dodd — poor chap, he is dead now, — and with my mother's old plaid shawl and a well-filled lunch basket, go off into the woods beyond the upper pond. The shawl made a capital tent, and after we had filled our bags with nuts we would build a roaring camp fire, boil tea in a tin pail, tell over the stories we had read of back-woods life, and altogether feel quite as if we were pioneers. Sometimes, too, we were lucky enough to catch a few small perch, or sun-fish, which we would take home proudly, at the end of a very long string. How plainly those days come back at the bare suggestion of the woods. Yes, I know I should enjoy it."

An hour later Moulton was given the opportunity of proving the sincerity of this last statement. He drove from the concert with the Whitneys, as their home was but a short distance from the Club, and at Helen's invitation stopped to be presented to Miss Seaton. That young lady met them at the door with an open note in her hand and said :

"Is this not wretched news, Helen, dear ? Mr. Kennedy has just sent me this note, in which he says that he has had a telegram requiring his immediate return to Cheyenne and must take the noon train to-morrow."

Helen looked at Moulton and blushed slightly as she caught his eye and saw that he read her thought.

"I am very sorry," she said, " for Mr. Kennedy, but perhaps we can find some self-sacrificing man willing to take his place."

"Shall I retire," asked Moulton ; "while you determine who the fortunate one shall be ? "

"Does that mean that you wish to escape ?" Helen asked.

"Not at all.   Nothing could give me greater pleasure than to be of your party, I assure you."

And so it was promptly decided that Moulton should take Kennedy's place.

CHAPTER II.

IT was nearly noon when the train that carried Ferris, stopped at the little town of Keating. Except for a few idle men lounging on the benches and for John Brent, the superintendent of the mine, who knew of his coming, the station was deserted, for this train stopped only on special order such as Ferris had obtained. But in front of the "Miner's Hotel," which stood a few hundred feet from the station, could be seen groups of rough looking men, and the coarse shouts and profanity from the bar-room showed that the poor man's worst enemy — rum — was making its influence felt. As the train slowed up most of these men lazily sauntered toward it.

"I think, sir, we had better get over to the mine as soon as possible for the men are in an ugly mood to-day;" said Brent, as he went to help the station agent with Ferris's trunk. It required but a moment to place the trunk on the back of the buck-board, but while Brent was securing it the vehicle was surrounded, and the

crowd found courage to show its ugly temper in
jeering remarks directed first at Brent and then,
emboldened by his silence, at Ferris. As Brent
took his seat beside Ferris and gathered up the
reins, a maudlin brute stood in front of the
horse and said :

"This here's the feller that telegraphed John
Brent to shet down the mine. Had n't we better give him a shakin' up while we 've got him,
boys ?"

As he spoke, he grasped the bridle of the
horse. The color came into Ferris's face as he
sprang quickly to his feet and placed his hand
on Brent's shoulder, for the latter had also
started to rise.

" Keep cool, John," he said, in an undertone,
and in the few seconds before he spoke again
the color of his face gave way to a fierce pale-
ness. In the sullen faces before him he read
the ugly temper of the crowd, but though he
realized how powerless he and Brent might be to
resist their violence, the thought of yielding
never entered his mind. Had he needed en-
couragement he might have found it in the face
of a horseman who at that moment crossed the
railway track from the direction of the woods
and quickly reined up a few feet from the crowd.
He was not a large man, but broad-shouldered
and deep-chested, and he sat in his saddle like a

trooper. The resemblance, too, was heightened by the cork helmet he wore and the rifle that hung from the pommel of his saddle. Ferris had never seen him before but in the brief glance he gave him he recognized a friend if one were needed.

Looking steadily at the man who held his horse's bridle, he spoke sharply :

"Stand aside there, or I will not answer for the consequences," he said with deliberation, but in a way and coupled with a look that caused the man to obey. Then he added in a scarcely milder tone: "Men, I have been sent here to determine for the owners whether the Gloria Mine shall start up or remain idle. You will not help me toward a decision favorable to you by acting as you have begun. Drive on, John."

The crowd parted to allow the buck-board to pass, as the horse sprang forward under the touch of the whip.

The Gloria Mine was about half a mile from the station, but the road was dotted with small houses nearly all the way to the ore yards, beyond which were the company's store, the office, the superintendent's house and the numerous other buildings usually found about a plant of this kind. By the time they reached the office Brent had fully outlined the situation of affairs, and it was plain to Ferris that something must be done at once.

The strike, which had now lasted nearly four months, was due to an order of the Board of Directors reducing the wages of the miners fifteen to twenty-five per cent. Ferris had opposed this reduction, but the Gloria stock had been so liberally watered at a time when the demand for iron ore seemed insatiable by reason of the building of many new railroads throughout the country and particularly in the west, that it was difficult to convince the owners of this stock that with a falling market their dividends should suffer rather than the miners' wages. Before the meeting of the directors at which the reduction was ordered, he had carefully prepared a table of figures which he regarded as an unanswerable argument in favor of a dividend reduction, and such indeed it should have been. But the soullessness of this particular corporation was exemplified in the person of a venerable director, one Grimshaw, who owned a large amount of the stock and controlled much more, as he did also in numerous other corporations. He did not attempt to disprove the facts stated by Ferris, but simply ignored them. He reminded the directors that the stock of the Gloria company was ten million dollars and that for the past ten years it had paid a dividend of

eight per cent; that while the demand for iron
ore had decreased, so also had the price of
food and clothing; that the miners were bene-
fited by the reductions in the price of commodi-
ties, and that therefore they could well afford to
work at the reduced scale of wages. Thereupon
it was declared to be the sense of the board of
directors that a reduction of fifteen to twenty-
five per cent. in all wages should be made, the
manager was ordered to construct a new wage
scale, the usual dividend was declared and the
meeting adjourned.

No one knew better than Ferris the hopelessness of attempting to get the men to accept the
new scale of wages, for a like reduction had
been made the year before, and very nearly resulted in the shutting down of the mine. At
that time, however, the same wage-scale was
adopted by all the neighboring mines, and the
reasons given by Grimshaw were then used and
their force exhausted. He was not surprised,
therefore, when a telegram from Brent announced that the men had almost unanimously
refused to accept the company's terms.

But Ferris was not easily discouraged. When
he realized, after the strike had continued for two
months, how unreasonable and hopeless it was to
expect the men to return at the reduced scale,
he conceived a plan that offered a possible solu-

tion of the trouble. He represented to the
directors the advisability of making extensive
repairs in the machinery of the mine while it
was idle, and of introducing certain modern ap-
paratus that would largely increase its output.
He did this with much doubt as to its success,
for when he had made the same proposition
some two years before, Grimshaw had opposed
him. But to his surprise this director was now
an earnest advocate of the improvements. Having gained this point, Ferris next revived the
wage question, and was allowed to prepare a new
scale based upon the reduction, but with authority to make a *pro rata* advance as the increased
production of the mine might warrant. He had
long cherished the plan of modernizing the
machinery of the Gloria mine, yet so long as the
dividends were satisfactory he was unable to impress upon the management the necessity of any
improvement in the plant. Now that Grimshaw
favored the plan, he was able to carry it out in
the most liberal way, and within a few weeks the
new machinery began to arrive at the mine
more rapidly than the mechanics could put it in
place.

When the inhabitants of Keating first saw
these repairs in progress they regarded it as a
sign that the company had decided to recon-
sider its action and resume work at the old scale

of wages; but latterly, as the repairs neared
completion, a new rumor had been started, to the
effect that when the machinery was in readiness
a full force of imported contract laborers would
be brought to work the mine. In vain Brent
denied this rumor, which, as it gained credence,
produced an ugly feeling, even among the few
men who had shown a disposition to accede to
the company's offer. Threats of destroying the
plant were made, until Brent realized that unless
some decisive steps were taken to allay the bad
feeling, it must soon find vent in some desper-
ate act.

After his arrival Ferris spent the two hours
before luncheon in inspecting the new machinery and repairs, giving occasional directions as
to slight changes, but, on the whole, finding
much satisfaction at the manner in which the
work had been done.

"I should scarcely recognize the old mine,"
said he to Brent, as they walked toward the
office; "and I believe that my estimates of increase of the output, which I confess at first
seemed rather exaggerated, will be exceeded if
the men have not been rendered utterly worth-
less by idleness and liquor."

"The men would be all right, sir, if you
could get them at work again, but I am afraid
you will find that harder than you think for."

"I cannot see why it should be. I can certainly convince the most doubtful of them that with our improved plant and with the new tonnage scale of wages, their pay cannot be less than it was before the strike, and it may be somewhat more."

"If you could get the men to listen to you and understand your plan, and particularly if you could make them see that you are working in their interest, I don't question that you could get them to come back upon your terms. But the fact is, these men think that they have been treated unfairly. As you know, many of them are foreigners, the majority are stupid and ignorant. During the past month, and particularly during the past week, the worst element has predominated, and even the older and better men, who have heretofore advised patience and moderation, seem to offer now no opposition to the incendiary plans of the hot-headed and malicious."

"They have not frightened you, surely, have they, John?" asked Ferris with a smile.

"No, sir, they have not frightened me; at least I am not afraid for my own safety, but four years' campaigning has taught me to appreciate danger when I see it, and I have lived long enough with these men to know their temper. Only night before last, Jack Smith, who has been working on the new double-hoist, ran across a gang of men down by the Corduroy bridge, as he was coming home from Burton's cabin, and as he doesn't stand in very high favor with them, he hid under the bridge to let them pass. They stopped on the bridge just over him, and he heard enough of their plans to satisfy him and me that matters were about as serious as they could well be. Black Tim was the leader of the gang and Jack heard him giving directions to some of the others as to how they would go about wrecking our plant in a way that did great credit to his cunning. Two of our men who were over at the Spencer mine, where it was supposed they had gone to seek work, sent word that they had secured enough dynamite to blow our whole outfit into eternity. The men moved on before Smith could get further information as to their plans, but I am satisfied that the devil is in them and liable to break out at any minute. While I was waiting for your train at the station this morning, I overheard Tim tell one of his men that the meeting for to-night would be at 9 o'clock. Now it may be only my suspicions, but the meetings have always been held at 7 and I don't regard the change as any good sign, particularly as Tim has come to be the principal speaker at the meetings held of late."

"Is there any one among the men from whom we can learn more of this meeting to-night?" Ferris asked after a brief silence.

"No, I think not," answered Brent. "The men, as you know, were almost unanimous in calling the strike, and while there were those who were willing to come back at the reduced scale, some of these have moved away and others have nothing to say against the bad element; they are simply cowed. It is possible," Brent added, "that Dr. Burton might throw some light on the matter, as he has been looking after some of the sick folks lately and may have got an inkling of what is going on."

"Do you think that this Dr. Burton would care or would dare to tell us of the plans of Black Tim's gang, if he knows anything concerning them?"

Brent smiled as he answered: "I can't say whether he would care to tell anything or not, but if he wanted to do so, it is not likely that he would be afraid. He is a powerful fellow, though he doesn't look it, and the men know it. Two weeks ago Sunday evening, he was called to see Black Tim's wife, who was at the point of death, and as he passed the hotel on his way to the shanty, he found Tim drinking whiskey and told him he had better go home. Tim's an ugly brute and a bully, as you know, and he didn't like being spoken to before the men. So he invited the doctor to go to hell. With that, Burton jumped off his horse and told him to defend himself. The men expected to see a fight, but there wasn't enough of it to be called that. Tim made a lunge at Burton and that was the end of the fight for him, for the doctor parried the blow with his right and knocked him down with his left, and as he rose, knocked him down again, left him insensible, and went off and spent the night at the bedside of the dying woman. No, I guess he is not much afraid."

"I think Burton is the man we need, and I wish that you would see that he gets this note at once;" and Ferris wrote as follows:

DEAR DR. BURTON:

I have come here with the hope of settling the strike in the interest of the men. I am satisfied that I can accomplish nothing unless they are diverted from their immediate plans to destroy our plant. May I not ask that you join me here at luncheon and aid us in reaching, if possible, a conclusion of this unfortunate trouble? Sincerely yours,

ROBERT FERRIS.

"Hadn't I better just send word that he is needed and ask him to come at once?" said Brent, as he gave the note to a boy, who had brought the mail from the post-office.

"No, John, that note will bring him if he is the man we want."

The boy galloped off with instructions to give the note with all speed into the doctor's hands. Burton was standing in front of the general store and postoffice, with one hand on his horse's mane and the other holding a letter which he was leisurely reading. He glanced at Ferris's note and said: "Say that I will come at once;" and then on second thought he added: "No, say that I will come immediately after luncheon." Then he crossed to the hotel, hitched his horse, and went into the bar-room, one end of which served as an eating-room for the few boarders and the occasional miners, lumbermen, peddlers and others that might have the misfortune and courage to partake of the meals served by the Widow Dooley, who was proprietress, cook, waitress, and general factotum of the place.

Hitherto Burton had paid but little attention to the conduct of the striking miners, contenting himself with giving assistance to such needy cases as were brought to his notice. He knew however, that the men regarded the manager as responsible in great measure for their trouble and hated him accordingly. He had never seen Ferris until his arrival two hours before, yet he liked his honest resolute face and believed whatever might be his plan for a settlement of the strike, it was at least worthy of serious consideration by the men, and he resolved to give him such assistance as might be within his power. He realized from what he had heard recently, that matters were nearing a crisis. As to just what that crisis was to be, he had given little thought. Now if he was to be of any assistance, he must gather some more definite information. As he entered the hotel, he found only a half dozen men, for the house had now but very few boarders.

There was little conversation during the dinner, which consisted of very old corned beef, cabbage and potatoes, and the only item of news that Burton gathered during the meal was that the superintendent of the Spencer mine had been robbed and beaten the night before, by two masked men, who disappeared in the direction of Keating. After the dinner one of the men, a young fellow not over twenty-five, whom Burton remembered to have seen and admired before he began to drink, handed Mrs. Dooley the price of his dinner and said: "This squares us up, Mrs. Dooley, and it's the last meal I shall have with you, for I am off for Marquette this afternoon. I have just enough money left to pay my fare, and if I stop any longer, I shall have to count the ties."

Burton was beginning to despair of learning here anything that might enlighten him concerning the immediate plans of the men.

"Let's have a last drink all around, boys, before Jack goes. The widow will set up the drinks this time, won't you, old woman? Jack's been a good customer of yours of late;" said one of the men.

"If there is enough liquor for the crowd, I will; but you know there is less than a pint of the stuff left, and the new keg won't get here till the 5 o'clock express from Marquette."

The last of the whisky was divided into six glasses, Burton having declined, and a parting health to Jack Turnley was drunk. The men then left the room and stood outside the doorway waiting to hear the whistle of the northbound train, which was about due. On the fly leaf of his diary Burton hastily wrote a note to the express agent at Denton, the next station north, stating that the supply of liquor in Keating was exhausted and that there were reasons of the utmost importance why no more should reach the town that night, and requesting him to detain at Denton the keg that had been shipped to Mrs. Dooley.

As he finished and addressed this note, he heard a coarse voice outside the door and recognized it at once as that of Tim Finney —

"Black Tim," as he was commonly called, because of his coarse, black hair, which almost met the heavy, black eyebrows growing straight across his forehead.

"You're a d—— fool, and a coward, to leave us now, Jack; wait until after to-night, and you can bet your life you will get back your old job at the mine. We are all pals here," Tim added, looking around cautiously; "and I don't mind telling you if you will keep your mouth shut, that we are going to learn John Brent and his young boss a lesson to-night that they will remember for a while." Then he added in a lower tone: "There is going to be an accident at the mine to-night and we'll show him that they can't starve us to death, and then run in a gang of nigger miners to take our jobs."

Burton heard Turnley protest that if he staid until morning, he would not have money enough to take him away, and he knew from the man's tone and from what he had seen of him before, that he did not altogether favor Tim's method of bringing the company to terms.

"Damn the money, boy; take this shiner, and if things don't turn out as I tell you then you can buy a ticket with it to-morrow."

There was an exclamation of surprise from the men as Tim produced a bright ten dollar gold piece.

"There is more where that came from, lads, and I tell ye the League will stand by us now if we show 'em that we have got the sand to do our duty."

Just then the whistle of the north-bound engine sounded, and Burton passed from the door, hurried to the station, and gave his note to the conductor, who promised to deliver it to the agent at Denton. The train moved off and as he returned to the hotel and mounted his horse, he noticed Jack Turnley standing with a look of shame upon his face, watching the train as it disappeared across the river and into the pines beyond.

As Burton rode up to the office at the mine, Ferris met him and introduced himself.

"It is very good of you to come, doctor, and knowing your interest in the men, I am sure that I do not need to make excuses for sending for you on a matter so entirely unprofessional."

"Pray don't mention it, Mr. Ferris. I am always glad to respond to an unprofessional call. It is the professional ones that distress me, for I no longer pretend to practice medicine and, indeed, have not done so for many years. I have succeeded until this summer in concealing from the people about here the fact that I am a physician; but when Dr. Jamieson left, he was unkind enough to disclose my professional identity to a chronic patient of his, and since then I have been unable to escape. I assure you that it will be a most happy relief to me when the men can afford to get Jamieson back."

As they entered the office, Brent joined them and the three went to a room on the second floor where they would not be overheard. What Burton had learned in the hour before, satisfied them that there was need for immediate action.

Ferris explained to Burton, as briefly as possible, the repairs that had been made at the mine and how, with the new tonnage scale, the wages of the men must equal or exceed what they had received before the strike. Burton readily comprehended the plan and its entire practicability, but he appreciated the difficulty at such a late hour, in getting it before the men in a convincing way.

The conference, which lasted nearly an hour, resulted in a plan by which Burton and Brent were to see such of the old workmen as might be reasonably disposed, and induce them to attend the meeting in the evening and listen to the proposition that Ferris would make. It was thought advisable also that the meeting should be called not later than half past seven, as the freight train from the north passed at half past eight, and Brent believed that it might bring some of the worst characters from Denton or the mines beyond.

Burton had not realized until he undertook this mission how many of the families in the little town were indebted to him in one way or another. Many of the men were away from their homes, but before nightfall he had succeeded in seeing at least fifty and had secured their promise to attend the meeting. He let it be known that he had had a conference with the manager and had given his promise that if Ferris would be present, the men would accord him a fair hearing. Not a few resented the suggestion of having Ferris speak to them; but for Burton's sake, they promised that even Ferris should have an opportunity to be heard if they could accomplish it. Although these fifty men were but a small minority of the men who had suffered from the strike, yet they were of the best, and with even so few to be depended upon, Burton hoped that the others might be led.

Nor was Brent idle during the afternoon, for while many of his men hated him as a servant of the company, there were others, particularly among the better class of miners, who knew that the reduction in their wages had been in the face of his earnest protest and that he had always been straightforward with them. Not a few of these promised that they would do what they could to give Ferris a fair chance to be heard. "But God help him, John," said one of these, "if what he's got to say ain't square and fair; for if it ain't, he'll never get away alive."

While Burton and Brent were thus engaged in the town, Ferris took such measures as were possible with the few men at the mine to protect the property if violence should be attempted. He armed the men that could certainly be trusted and arranged that they should guard the buildings and the shaft, but the ore yard was, unfortunately, exposed. It was of triangular shape; on one side of it the river ran, and, forming an angle with the river, was an old shaft, or rather tunnel, that ran under the river, dipping but a slight distance below its bed. The bulk of the ore remaining in the yard lay in a giant pile in this angle; if the base of the wall that guarded it were broken on one side, a great part of the ore would slide into the river, and if a breach were made on the other side, it would fall into the abandoned tunnel and the worked out level below, letting in the river, if its bank were broken also. But Ferris did not believe that this point which was so exposed would be attacked, and concluded, after looking over the yard, that the most vulnerable place was the switch tracks and trestle work that led across the river and into the yard, and here he stationed the only two men that could be spared from the guard of the buildings. At six o'clock he had completed his work, and as he returned to the office he met the boy who had come with the mail.

"The south-bound express is late, Willie," Ferris said, as the little fellow dismounted from his pony with the mail-bag.

"No, sir, the train was on time," the boy answered; "but there came near being an awful fight at the depot. Mrs. Dooley 'spected a keg of whiskey on the train and it didn't come, and she got a lot of men to hold the train and search the express car and the baggage car. The express agent locked himself in the car and they busted the door in with a railroad tie. I guess the agent thought they were going to rob his safe, for he fired into the crowd, and I reckon poor Jack Turnley was hurt bad, 'cause the load struck him, and when I come away Doc Burton was picking the buckshot out of him. Will you want me for awhile, Mr. Ferris? Doc said he would like to have me at the hall at half-past seven."

"No; go and get your supper, and do not fail to meet Dr. Burton," answered Ferris as he went into the office.

"O, I won't, sir; there's going to be an awful

big meeting at the hall to-night;" and the boy galloped off to the barn.

After supper Ferris returned to the office and waited impatiently for some word from the town. Eight o'clock came and no message from Burton or Brent, and from that time until nine, he walked restlessly in front of the office door. He had decided to wait no longer, and was just starting toward the town when he heard the sharp clatter of the pony's hoofs, and in a moment the mail-boy stopped before him. The little fellow was bareheaded, and down his face a quick stream of blood was flowing from a wound above the temple. By the bright moonlight Ferris could see that he was deadly pale from fright or loss of blood.

"Quick, Mr. Ferris," he said faintly, holding fast to the pommel of his saddle, "they want you at the hall. Black Tim and his men are coming up the river road. O, stop them, Mr. Ferris, or they will do something awful, for they've got two great cans of powder."

He tried to dismount, but would have fallen had not Ferris caught him. Taking the child in his arms, he ran with him to Brent's house, where Mrs. Brent, hearing his step upon the porch, met them at the door. Ferris laid the child on the lounge, and pressing together the wound, checked the loss of blood.

"Hurry, hurry, Mr. Ferris; they are coming. Don't you hear them? Don't you hear them? O, sir, don't mind me. I—I—;" and the little voice was silent.

"You need not wait, Mr. Ferris; I will look after Willie," said Mrs. Brent; and Ferris, knowing that no care that he might give could add to her motherly tenderness, hurried from the house.

As he passed the engine house he ordered Pat, the faithful old fireman stationed there, to come with him, and the two ran along the side of the ore yard toward the road up which he knew that Tim and his men must come. At the end of the yard they stopped, and, looking cautiously around the corner of the great pile past which the road ran, Ferris saw the crowd of vandals moving rapidly toward them.

"Stand close to the wall, Pat," he said. "Be ready to shoot, but do n't fire until I tell you. If we have to fire, don't shoot at Tim. I will take care of him. Steady now; they're almost here."

The tramp of heavy feet on the hard road could now be plainly heard as they neared the corner of the pile.

"Give me the big can and a fuse, Dutchy," they heard Tim say, as they stopped a moment, now less than thirty feet away. "I'll plant it around the corner by the mouth of the old tunnel, and the other we'll put under this end of the trestle bridge. They'll think hell's busted when they both go off."

Ferris knew, from this move, that Tim was not expecting opposition or he would not have cumbered himself with the dynamite can, but would have left his hands free to use his revolver, which he always carried. In a moment they moved forward again. As they reached the corner Ferris stepped quickly in front of them and thrust his revolver into Tim's face, while Pat covered with his rifle the men who closely followed their leader.

"Hold on to that can with both hands," Ferris said sharply, as Tim leaned over to place the can upon the ground. "Pat, shoot the first man that moves a hand."

There were six men in the party, and for an instant Ferris was at a loss to determine his next move; then he asked:

"Pat, do you know these men?"

"Sure, sor, every mother's son of thim, and a bad lot they be, sor," Pat replied.

"Do they all belong here?"

"Saving the two Murpheys and Dutchy, what belongs in Denton, and the scum of the town they be, sor. The Murpheys are the lads with their caps drawed down over their eyes; and Dutchy's the ugly devil I'm holding me gun on; and I'd thank ye, sor, for the order to shoot."

Looking at them, but still covering Tim with his revolver, Ferris said: "I will give you three men just two minutes to get out of rifle range. Take the Denton road and lose no time about it. Run."

They needed no second order, and in a few moments had disappeared in the pines through which the road led. Ferris then ordered Tim and the other man who carried the dynamite cans, to place them on their heads, and hold them there with both hands.

"Search this man, Pat, and if he or either of the others makes a move, it will be his last."

In a moment Pat had taken from Tim's hip pocket a heavy revolver, and in his search found a massive gold watch.

"That's a fine watch for the likes of ye to be carrying; and I suppose it's your monegram that's marked on the back," he added, as he held it up to the moonlight.

Tim's massive frame trembled and his face grew pale.

"Pat, put that back," he said fiercely, "or by hell, I'll kill ye. 'Twas give to me by a gentleman and it's mine."

"And the gent's dead now, I suppose."

"Put back the watch, Pat, and keep the revolver," said Ferris. " Now search the others."

But neither of these was armed.

" Now we will go to the town hall," was Ferris's next order. " Move on and be quick about
it."

With Tim and his companions in the advance, and Ferris and Pat following about
twenty feet distant, they moved at a quick gait
toward the main part of the town. When within a few hundred feet of the hall, Ferris met
Brent coming rapidly toward them. He saw
the situation at a glance.

" In heaven's name, Mr. Ferris, where did
you catch these devils ? But leave them to me
and get to the hall as fast as possible, for Burton
cannot hold the men ten minutes longer."

Ferris put up his revolver and ran. As he
neared the hall, he could hear Burton's voice
above the din, for it was evident that his hearers
had become impatient.

" I promise you, men, that he will be here in
ten minutes, if he has not been murdered on
the road," were the words that greeted him as
he rushed into the open doorway. And, although he was not conscious of it, his appearance indicated that probably he had narrowly
escaped the fate Burton had suggested, for his

collar and shirt had been stained with the blood of the mail-boy as he carried him in his arms.

Instantly all was silent. Burton was standing on the low platform at the end of the hall, and seeing Ferris enter, called: "This way, Mr. Ferris," in a tone of exultation. But as Ferris approached he saw the blood stains and his voice changed.

"My God, have they tried to kill you?" he asked anxiously. "Are you badly hurt?"

Then, for the first time, Ferris noticed the blood upon his clothing and remembered the little fellow whose life had perhaps already passed away. He paused an instant as he stepped to the platform and turned toward the men; but in that instant he saw in many of these rough faces a look of interest or rather, anxiety,— such as the sight of unjust human suffering will bring to men who at heart are just, even if that suffering be in those they hate.

"Men," he began with suppressed emotion, "these stains are from the blood of a little child, whom but a short time ago you sent to bring me to this hall. The faithful boy delivered your message, but he was waylaid and beaten, and it may be by this time that he has passed to his reward. I carried him in my arms."

Cries of "Shame, shame. Who did it? Lynch them," came from all parts of the hall.

Then Ferris told briefly and simply the occurrences of the preceding half hour, and it was plain that the majority did not favor such practical application of brute force, however they may have approved of it in theory.

"But," he proceeded, "it is not to tell you of these things that I am here to-night. I am here to consider with you the unfortunate situation, and with you to determine how it may best be ended."

The changes and improvements in the plant were then explained at length and the possibilities of a largely increased output were demonstrated to a certainty. It was shown how, with a tonnage scale of wages, the pay of the men would, in all probability, equal, if it did not exceed, that received before the strike.

In conclusion he said: "I know that many of you hold me responsible for the suffering that has come to you during the past four months, I can only tell you that I am not. But however you may feel toward me, I want you to consider carefully, before you decide to-night, the facts I have stated, and realize that the responsibility is now with you to determine whether the Gloria mine shall remain shut down, or prosperity shall come again to this town. If you have no questions to ask me that will make the matter plainer, I will go and leave you to decide what you think is for your best interest. Should you conclude to return to work, we will start up day after to-morrow. Good-night."

There was a slight murmur of approval, as Ferris and Burton walked down the hall, and as they passed out the door Burton said: "Mr. Ferris, I congratulate you, for you have won."

"Thank you, doctor, but without your help I fear it would have been otherwise."

As they returned to the mine Burton gave Ferris a brief account of his afternoon and evening's work.

"But," he said, as they neared Brent's house, where Burton wished to see the injured child, "I have been well repaid, for this has been the most instructive day of my life. Most of our lessons in the intense of human passion are learned from books, where the facts are largely the creatures of the imagination. To-day I have had a lesson in realism that has run the gamut of every passion."

"Except love," Ferris added rather sarcastically.

"No, I have had a glimpse of that, too. It lasted but a moment, but it was real. While I was dressing Turnley's wounds, a young woman — so young that I thought her a mere child, at first glance — stood very near to me. I was attracted by the pallor of her face, and as I

glanced at times from my work, I could see
that she was laboring under intense emotion.
Her hands were clasped tightly across her
breast and her lips quivered. Several times I
found it necessary to use the knife rather
severely, and each tremor of pain had its reflex
in her face. As I finished my work the poor
fellow began to lose consciousness and talked
incoherently. The woman leaned forward to
catch each faint word, though it was plain she
was striving to conceal from the crowd her
heart's secret. But in vain. I heard my patient
call, ' Molly.' Instantly the woman was on
her knees at his side. ' Yes, yes, Jack, I am
here, darlin',' was all she said, yet the touch of
her hand, roughened by hard work, but softened
by love, will do more to win Jack Turnley back
to life than all my surgery ! "

CHAPTER III.

WHEN Captain Vinton reached Chicago on the morning after Ferris's departure he found Moulton awaiting him at the railway station. The latter, after leaving the Whitneys the night before, had spent some hours in packing his bags and, with the aid of a book entitled, " How to Camp Out," had made a list of the things that he thought might be needed for his outing. As he read these off to Vinton after they had gone to Ferris's rooms, the old fellow fairly shook with laughter.

" My dear boy," he said, when Moulton had finished, " throw the list away, I beg of you. It may be all right for camping on Lake George and in proximity to a summer hotel, but for Northern Michigan such *impedimenta* would be the veriest rubbish. Throw out the percale shirts and the whisk broom and the blacking brush and the wash ties. In fact, throw the whole thing away and I will tell you what to take."

And Moulton found that from his wardrobe and Ferris's store room he was able to supply all that Vinton deemed necessary and much more, and when he had re-packed his bags he still had ample room for the things that Ferris had left for Vinton, but which the latter declined to be "bothered with."

In the evening they dined at the Whitneys, and there Moulton learned from Miss Seaton more definitely the location of the camp, and was delighted to discover that it was only twenty miles from Keating.

"I will drop a line to Ferris before we go," he said ; "and with your permission will urge him to spend a day with us before he returns to the city."

"And I will add a postscript," said Vinton, "for I am most anxious to see him. We have not in years been separated so long a time before."

"But pray do not restrict his visit to one day," Miss Seaton said ; "for although from Keating to Round Lake is only twenty miles by the map, the trail is not a good one, and whether the distance be covered on foot or by the river, it means at least one day's hard travel. My uncle, Dr. Burton, has a cabin eight miles from Keating, and it would be well for Mr. Ferris to break the journey by stopping with him. Mention this in your note, for I can assure you that Uncle Tom will welcome him most warmly."

And so before starting for the train, Moulton mailed his letter to Ferris, with a succession of postscripts by Vinton, Whitney, and Helen.

When Escanaba was reached early the next morning, the party went at once from the station to Colonel Elting's tug boat, on the deck of which breakfast was served as they steamed out of the harbor. In a direct line the little town of Sturgeon, where the lumber mill was located and from which wagons were to take the campers into the woods, was distant from Escanaba only fifteen miles, but by water the wide circuit around Squaw Point added six more, and it was eleven o'clock before they ran beneath the tall piles of lumber on the docks and heard the welcoming blast from the steam whistle of the mill.

There is something fascinating about a modern saw-mill, even to one not familiar with machinery. The mechanism is so wonderfully rapid and precise, and yet so simple and exposed that anyone can readily see how perfectly the vast power of the steam engine is made responsive to the human hand. And what better instance of practical agility can be found than that shown by yonder tall, lank fellow in a red flannel shirt, with trousers tucked into his red woolen socks, who, with pike-pole in hand, lightly steps from log to log as they bob and turn in the water beneath his weight? Notice with what consummate skill he selects the desired log, and, standing erect, rides it to the elevator chains that run it up the incline to the log-deck, where iron arms throw it upon the carriage. Then, too, there is an excitement in watching the sawyer holding fast to the lever of the carriage as it dashes the log into the path of the spinning saw-blade, changing its idle hum to a fierce shriek, and then rushes back for a new charge, pausing only long enough to permit fingers of steel quickly to turn the log or set it forward.

"Modern invention has wrought wonderful changes in the saw-mill, has it not?" said Vinton to Colonel Elting, as they walked up the quarter-mile of saw-dust road that led from the mill to the town.

"Indeed, it has," he answered. "When I was a boy my father had a lumber mill down in Maine. It was driven by water-power, and had a single muley saw. When the log was once set it was simply a question of time when the carriage would reach the end of the track. With the machinery you have just seen I cut more lumber in a day than the old mill could cut in a year."

After a short rest and a hearty luncheon, the start for the woods was made in two buck-

boards, with a light wagon to carry the luggage.
The country for the first five miles of the journey was covered with a second growth of pine or
small hardwood, · and except for occasional
glimpses of the river along which the wagon
road ran, the view was altogether uninteresting.
Then, after a half mile of "corduroy" road
through a tamarack swamp, they passed on to a
hardwood ridge, and the beauty of the northern
woods began to unfold itself.

Miss Seaton had made the journey many
times before, and watched with amusement the
expression of disappointment that had settled
upon her companions during the first tedious
hour's ride disappear as they went at a brisk trot
along the stretches of good road beneath inter-
lacing branches of maple and beech and elm
that protected them from the heat of the September sun.

"This is really beautiful, Madge," said
Helen, after a half hour's drive had begun to
give her some assurance that the change of
scenery was permanent. "Will it be like this all
the way to camp ?"

"Yes, with only an occasional uninteresting
spot to emphasize the beauty of the rest. We
will stop for a half hour at the first rapids, which
we should reach very soon, and perhaps I can

initiate you into the blessed mystery of trout
fishing, if we can conveniently get some flies and
a line."

"I have those in the top of my hand bag.
You know Mr. Kennedy sent me his fly-book
and reel, poor fellow;" and, finding the bag beneath the seat, Helen gave the reel and book to
Madge, who selected a cast of sombre color.

The rapids at which the stop was made were
at a sharp bend of the river, the bed of which
was filled for a hundred yards or more with a
mass of rocks which the persistent stream had
cut from the steep bank. Over and around
these the water rushed and whirled in its noisy
haste to reach the placid current below. Quickly
jointing her rod, Madge took Helen down
stream a short distance to a point where the
descent to the water was easy, while Moulton
stood on the bank watching them and struggling
with a new pipe which Vinton had assured him
better harmonized with the woods than did a
cigar. He had just abandoned the undertaking
and lighted a cigar, when Vinton joined him.

"I find, Captain," he said, "that anatom-
ically I am unfitted for smoking a pipe. One
really needs a leather tongue, a cast iron stomach, and infinite lung power to do it with any
degree of success or satisfaction. Watch those

girls," he added, pointing to Helen and Madge ;
"they are very picturesque, but have you an idea
that they will catch anything ?"

"I have great confidence in Miss Seaton's
skill with the rod, yet I confess that in this
strong sunlight I should not look for success."

Scarcely had he spoken, however, when
Madge was seen cautiously to cast down stream
in such manner that her flies were whirled into
a little pool near the shore and beneath the deep
shadow of an overhanging beech tree. Along
the surface of the water the flies were skipped
back only to be cast again nearer to the shore
and this time there was a quick response and the
light rod doubled as the trout darted into midstream. In an instant Vinton was all excitement.

"Why doesn't she pull him in ?" said Moulton, impatiently, as he watched the line reeled
slowly in and allowed to run out again whenever
the fish made a fresh dash for freedom.

"Experience will teach you the reason better
than any words." Vinton replied.

Madge had stepped from the shore onto a
flat boulder in the stream and now swung the
line within reach of Helen, who by a vigorous
jerk landed the exhausted trout high amid the
bushes on the bank. Disentangling the line,
Helen now tried her skill and after several failures was rewarded with two smaller fish and

finally with one "two-pounder" (actual weight one pound and a quarter), that revenged itself by breaking the tip of the rod.

An hour more of easy driving and a short detour from the main road, brought the party in sight of Round Lake at its eastern side and nearly opposite the camp. The sun was just sinking behind the great trees, in the shadow of which the white tents and a single cabin could be dimly seen. At no time of day is a wood's lake so gorgeously beautiful as at sunset, when the quiet water mirrors the glory of the heavens above and reflects in perfect outline the trees that border the shore ; and to the traveler, wearied with a long day's journey, the sight of camp with its slender thread of smoke rising to dissipate itself in the overhanging branches is as welcome as was the vision of Canaan to the children of Israel.

Around the edge of the lake was a newly made road—if the mere cutting out of the trees could be dignified with that name—which was so rough that a walk along the hard sandy beach was thought by all preferable. As they started thus the sharp blows of an axe could be heard echoing around the shore, notwithstanding the lake was nearly a mile in width. Presently these sounds ceased and a canoe was seen to put out from the shore with a single figure kneeling in it and driving it rapidly toward them with swift strokes of his paddle.

"That is Charley, our Indian," said Madge, after watching him a moment. "How beautifully he handles a canoe. He has only one superior in these woods. That is his brother Joe, my Uncle's man."

"Have you had him as a guide before?" Vinton asked.

"Oh, yes, many times. Both he and his brother are devoted to Uncle Tom and are with him always when he is in the woods. In the winter and spring they live with their families in the little Indian village near Sturgeon."

As she finished speaking Madge gave a loud, peculiar call, which the Indian evidently recognized, for his answer came almost like an echo. A few minutes later the canoe neared the beach in front of them, and stepping into the water, Charley drew the boat ashore. He was above the average height, straight as an arrow, and except for his complexion, might have passed for a full-blooded Indian instead of a half-breed. His delight at seeing Madge again was unmistakable and he grasped her hand warmly while she spoke a few words to him in Chippewa. As he was presented to the others he simply said, "Howdy," nodding his head to each. The canoe was a "dug-out," but a perfect specimen of the Indian's handiwork, light and safe enough if one sat very still.

"Won't you take Mrs. Elting and Helen to the camp in the canoe, Mr. Moulton?" Madge asked. "It will easily carry three."

Moulton looked at the slender craft and shook his head.

"Thank you, Miss Seaton, but I fear it would be too risky. If it were fitted with outriggers and a pair of oars I could confidently manage it. With the paddle I am an utter novice."

As Vinton also expressed a preference for *terra firma*, Madge volunteered to take Mrs. Elting and Helen over, and with evident misgivings they consented to go.

Charley pushed the canoe from shore, with Helen in the bow and Madge kneeling in the stern, and after watching them a moment he turned to Vinton, and said: "Madge paddle canoe like Injun. Joe and me teach her years ago."

The camp was soon reached and the tents were found pitched on the bluff some thirty feet above the water's edge. At this point the timber was free from underbrush and consisted mainly of maple, beech and hemlock, with here and there a pine that towered above the surrounding foliage. The cabin of rough hewn logs stood about a hundred feet from the edge

of the bluff and on one side of it were pitched
a small tent for Vinton and a larger one for
Whitney and Moulton, while on the opposite
side were the tent for Mrs. Elting, Madge and
Helen, the dining tent (somewhat nearer the
lake), the cook tent and the sleeping tent for the
cook and guide. The cabin itself had been
reserved as a general living room and as a sleeping room for the ladies in event the weather
proved very bad. Down the face of the bluff
ran a flight of steps to the beach, and at this
point several logs had been staked in the shallow water to serve as a landing for the fleet,
which consisted of two canoes and a cedar boat
fitted with oars.

When the men reached the camp they found
Madge and Helen seated on a bench at the edge
of the bluff and in front of a goodly pile of
wood that had been laid in readiness for the
first camp fire.

" Did you ever imagine anything more beautiful and comfortable than this ? " said Helen to
Vinton, as she and Madge walked with him from
one tent to another. "I had supposed that we
were to sleep on hemlock boughs and dine off
tin plates and depend for our cooking upon
an open fire and a frying pan. But, thanks to
Madge and Colonel Elting, we have comfortable
beds to rest our weary bodies and clean white

dishes and a regular kitchen stove. This is indeed luxury in the heart of the wilderness."

"Do you approve of it, Captain?" Madge asked. "Or are you one of those veteran campers who scorn all suggestion of civilization when they come into the woods?"

"I have yet to learn," Vinton answered, "that the pleasures of camping can be lessened by a comfortable bed or by having one's food well cooked and decently served. The somniferous virtue of the hemlock boughs is not destroyed by laying a mattress on top of them as you have done, and the frying pan is an abomination anywhere. Certainly the cook stove will save Dan'l much profanity in windy weather."

At the dining tent they were welcomed by Dan'l, an old Irishman whom Vinton had contributed as cook for the party, and whom he had sent from the east several days before.

"Dan'l is a queer old fellow," Vinton said, as they left him setting the table for dinner. "He was with me for several years during the war, and when I left the Navy, insisted on following me. He is a very fair cook and can do any kind of housework. Indeed, I find him well nigh indispensable."

An hour later Dan'l demonstrated to the satisfaction of all that at least he was not a novice in the kitchen, and the dinner of trout, bass and partridges, with a dessert of wild cranberry tarts, might well have tempted even less voracious appetites.

To one who loves the woods, nothing is more delightful, restful or comforting than a camp fire on an autumn night. Aside from its genial warmth there is something about it that appeals to every temperament and mood. If you are grave or weary you may draw your top coat over your shoulders and build castles in the glowing embers beneath the blazing logs. If your spirits are light you can watch the tongues of flame as they chase the sparks in their upward flight to the branches overhead. Or if ill-humor possesses you, you may safely vent it by poking the fire, feeling sure that its smouldering resentment will soon die out.

Around such a fire the party gathered after dinner and soon began to discuss the plans for the morrow. Whitney and Vinton, enthusiastic hunters always, having seen numerous signs of deer on the road to camp, were desirous of making an early start in search of game. Madge had learned from Charley that very few deer had been seen in the immediate vicinity of the lake, this being due, as he thought, in part to the noise at the camp, but mainly to the fact that there were wolves about. A few days before, however, he had been at Elk Lake, some six miles distant, and believed that much better shooting could be had there.

It was agreed, therefore, that in the morning the men should go with Charley to Elk Lake, taking with them a shelter tent and provisions so that they could remain over night, and, if they failed to get a deer during the day they might be sure of finding one with a head-light before the moon came up.

"Night hunting is simply butchery," Madge said to Whitney, as she saw him putting his head-light in order; "but perhaps it is justifiable until we have meat in camp. I trust that you will at least use a rifle if you do find it necessary to shoot at night."

"I confess that I had planned to be more barbarous," he answered, "and had loaded some shells with buckshot; but I will throw them out. How will you and Mrs. Elting and Helen amuse yourselves while we are gone?"

"We shall be very busy, no doubt. Mrs. Elting and Helen can provide the larder with fish, and I hope to add a few partridges and ducks. Besides, I must renew my acquaintance with some of my old haunts. There will be much to fill our time until you return. The days are never too long in camp."

Moulton reluctantly consented to join the expedition to Elk Lake.

"This sudden display of energy does not appeal to me at all," he said, as he returned from his tent with his banjo, having left Whitney and Vinton to make the preparations for the journey. "I had looked forward to a lazy, restful day tomorrow, such a day as I have not had in the woods since we were children in dear old Leamington."

"Do you remember that time?" Helen asked. "It seems very long ago to me."

Moulton paused a moment and then answered: "Do I remember? Listen." And in a low, sweet voice he sang a quaint, simple, old song that as children they had learned years before.

"What blessed memories that song revives," Helen said, with a sigh, as he finished. "It is very sweet. Why have you never sung it for me before."

"It is scarcely a classic," Moulton answered with a smile; "and I had supposed that your musical evolution had so far advanced that you would not care for such an old-fashioned tune. Intrinsically, of course, there is nothing to it, but I cannot tell you the comfort it has brought to me at times when I have been depressed — indigestion, you will say — and when childhood seemed to hold all that was honest in life."

"I can understand the feeling. Anyone can who truly loves music. I, too, have an old song—

Merrick calls it my morbid song — that is a comforter to me beyond everything else. When the demon of despondency possesses me I turn to the dear old song and it brings an infinite sense of peace and rest."

" Won't you sing it for me ? "

" Oh, no, indeed. At least not to-night. I am far from the mood for it now."

During the half hour that followed, Moulton and Helen sat alone in front of the fire. Mrs. Elting wished to write some letters, and Vinton and Whitney were packing their bags and making ready for the morrow. The old song had given the key note to their conversation and together they reviewed scenes that each thought the other had long since forgotten. An open wood fire, always conducive to reminiscence, is never so much so as with the accompaniment of old music.

In a way, Moulton had seen much of the Whitneys since his arrival in Chicago five years before, but at that time Helen was in the very whirl of society and he was seldom with her alone. As a child, he had been devoted to her above all others and it was no little disappointment to him to find himself sharing with many the friendship that years before he had in great measure monopolized. But this night, as they sat together on a low rustic bench mounted upon

rude rockers, the vanity and hollowness of
society were as far away from them as were its
devotees.

"What a rejuvenator this woods life must
be," Moulton said at last. "I certainly do not
feel over eighteen to-night, and, alas! I am
twenty-eight. I remember when that seemed at
least middle age to me. Fortunately our divi-
sions of life change with the point of view."

"It is inconsiderate of you to suggest approaching age at such a time," Helen answered.
"A moment ago I might have thought myself a
girl of fifteen but you remind me that I must
add a decade."

"Then let us forget our arithmetic in childish
fashion, or at least the sum of our years, and for
the next month measure time by our feelings
only. You are fifteen and I eighteen again."
And as he spoke Moulton found himself wish-
ing that the flight of time might indeed turn
backward so far.

Vinton was the first to join them, and as he
did so he said: "Come down to the landing if
you would see a beautiful view. The moon is
just rising above the pines on the opposite
shore."

Helen ran to the tent for Mrs. Elting and
Madge and together they followed Vinton and
Moulton. The sky was almost without a cloud,

and there was just enough wind to ripple the
path of light across the surface of the lake and
bend the slender rushes that rose from the shallow water. The eastern shore was black with
the deep shadows of the trees, but where the
light fell the white beach gleamed, with here
and there some fallen giant of the forest lying
across it, while all around the shore others lifted
high their arms in sharp silhouette against the
sky. So still was the night that the jumping of
the fish far out in the lake broke the quiet, and
the occasional crackling of the fire logs was as
distinct as a pistol shot. From the woods far
beyond the opposite shore the "Whoo; whoo-
whoo; whoo-whoo" of an owl came like the
cry of a human voice, causing Helen to ask in a
whisper :

"Did you hear that, Madge? Is it some one
lost ?"

"No, Helen dear, that is the voice of one
who is never lost in the night. It is the 'lord
of the midnight wood,' as Barry Cornwall calls
him — the hoot owl. His grewsome cry may be
a love song to his mate or perhaps a fierce chal-
lenge to some rival in her affections miles away.
You must get accustomed to this nightingale of
the northern woods, for he is no respecter of
slumber and you may hear his call from the tree
above your tent. Let us go to bed in the hope

that to-night, at least, we may be spared his serenade."

As they returned from the landing, good-night was said, and within a half hour the camp was hushed except for the occasional snapping of the fire, the flickering light of which cast fantastic shadows on the tents.

CHAPTER IV.

B Y noon of the day after his arrival in Keating, Ferris had completed his inspection of the works and was ready to start for Chicago, but on the receipt of Moulton's letter, he decided to spend a few days at Round Lake Camp before his return. Burton had passed the night with him at Brent's house, and having waited for the mail, joined his urgent invitation to Moulton's. The trail that they were to take led through the woods on the side of the town opposite the mine, and as they rode down the single street they saw many changes betokening the return of industrial life to the place. The men had apparently put off their slothful habits in the night and were busying themselves in work that must be done before the following day. The women sang through their household duties and the children shouted in their play as if the wolf of starvation which had prowled about their dwellings for months, had already been driven from the door ; and if the horsemen could have heard the many benedictions that were given them as they rode along, it might

73

have sorely endangered their modesty. But it was enough for Ferris to know that he had accomplished his work and was at last understood by his men, while Burton found ample recompense in the opportunity that had been given him to "observe phases of human character under somewhat peculiar conditions," as he expressed it.

Leaving the town, they passed on to an old logging road that ran through a long stretch of Norway pines. The narrow road was but little used except by Burton and was covered with pine needles, with here and there an open place in which the sunlight encouraged the berry bushes and grass. Under the heat of the afternoon sun the air was laden with the incense of the pines, and Ferris again and again breathed long and deep as if to crowd from his lungs the last vestiges of the bad air and soot of the city.

"Is it not too bad that we cannot have such air as this in our cities, where the great mass of the people must overwork to keep soul and body together?" he said, as they rode side by side.

"As a humanitarian, I say yes," replied Burton, "although it would be disastrous to my profession. Has it never struck you as remarkable, the disregard with which the matter of pure air is treated? It is a singular inconsistency of our race. We may be exceedingly careful, superficially, at least, as to the cleanliness and purity of our food and drink and clothing, and yet when it comes to that which is most essential to the nourishment of life, the air we breathe, we are strangely indifferent. Of course there is much time in the life of a city man or woman in which the lungs must be taxed in screening and straining bad air, but on the other hand, there is much time spent, particularly by the well-to-do, under conditions in which pure air is a possibility."

"You have evidently decided views in regard to ventilation."

"Yes, and yet I was not thinking of ventilation merely, but rather of purification. Ventilation is, of course, a good thing even if we simply supply fresh bad air in place of stale bad air. But how much better and more reasonable it would be to filter and purify the air we supply to our lungs precisely as we filter the water that we furnish our stomachs when its purity is questionable. Take, for example, two hotels in the heart of a great city, would you or any sane person hesitate in choosing between them if one supplied its sleeping rooms, its reading room and its dining room with purified air, while the other did not? And the matter is quite easy of accomplishment, and at surprisingly small cost. I gave this no little thought years ago, but I found in the end that the problem had been practically solved long before and that the trouble lay chiefly in the failure of the public to profit by its solution."

In the three hours' ride from the town to Burton's cabin, the two men learned much of each other. They were enough alike in many respects to be thoroughly congenial, yet different enough to be mutually interesting. Ferris had imagined that Burton probably had wealth sufficient to warrant his giving up the practice of his profession and spending most of his time in the woods or in travel. But he found that he was anything but an idler, and that his familiarity with current scientific matters proved him an earnest student of affairs.

Burton's cabin,— or rather cabins, for there were two,—stood a few rods from the bank of the stream, along which the trees had been cleared away, except a few at the water's edge. The cabins were not set *vis-à-vis*, in the conventional manner of logging camps, but both fronted on the clearing and stood about a hundred feet apart. The smaller was divided into two rooms, one serving as a sleeping room for Adam, the negro cook, and Joe, the Indian guide, and the other as kitchen and dining room. The larger cabin had three apartments. The front one was Burton's bed room ; back of this were two smaller rooms, one communicating with the front room and the other cut off from it and entered only by a side door. This last was the guest room. Burton called the apartment leading from his bed room, his work shop, but it was in truth a well equipped laboratory.

After they had dismounted and Ferris had put away his saddle bags and rod, Burton invited him to inspect the place. They first entered the kitchen, where Adam, in white cap and apron, went about his work of preparing the dinner like a veteran *chef.*

"I don't think that Adam approves of the woods," said Burton, as they left the kitchen. "He protests each year against coming, yet refuses to be left at home. He was raised by my father and seems to feel a paternal interest in me, and although he must be nearly sixty he is energetic beyond any negro I ever knew, and knows how to cook."

As they left the kitchen they saw Joe coming from the woods with a shotgun in one hand and a brace of grouse in the other. He was not a full-blooded Indian, although nearly as dark. His eyes were large, his hair was finer and he was shorter and more thick-set than his Chippewa brethren.

"This is my man Friday," said Burton to Ferris, as Joe came toward them. "Joe, my friend Mr. Ferris wants some fishing and you must get it for him to-morrow."

"Yes, I find him, Tom," replied Joe, delighted at the suggestion of a trip on the river. "Big trout down by rapids. Big buck, too, if him want one."

"What a blood-thirsty fellow the red man is," said Burton, as they walked across to the other cabin, while Joe took his game to the kitchen. "As long as there is a drop of Indian blood, you are sure to find an instinctive desire to slaughter game. Still, I am gradually civilizing Joe; he has learned to appreciate the difference between fishing with a rod and fly and using the old-fashioned pole and line, and is ready to admit that still-hunting with a 40-82 rifle is a more worthy way to kill deer than night-hunting with a musket and buckshot. Most of the trophies in this room," added Burton, as they entered his sleeping room, "are the work of Joe's rifle."

Ferris gave an exclamation of delight and surprise as he looked about the room. The floors were covered with skins of bear, deer, otter, and other fur animals found in the woods and streams thereabouts, and on the walls were several fine deer heads and horns, while over the stone fireplace hung the head of a buck elk. The furniture consisted of several chairs of rustic pattern,

a table, a book-case, a dressing-case and a bed
of heavy and simple design.

"You did not kill this in these woods, surely?"
said Ferris, after examining the head to satisfy
himself that it was indeed an elk.

"No," replied Burton, "I did not kill it,
yet it was killed about twelve years ago within
twenty miles of this spot. It must have been
the last of its kind in these parts for I have never
heard of one having been seen on the peninsula
since, and it was supposed that they had been
killed off or driven out long before. It was shot
by a little girl, my niece, then only fourteen
years old. You will meet her to-morrow when
you go to Round Lake, but you must not speak
of this head before her."

"I should think she might well be proud of
such a trophy."

"On the contrary, she is very much ashamed
of it, and after I had the head mounted, declined
to have it in our house. The fact is, she is a
stickler for the ethics of the chase, and as she
shot it in the water, she does not like to be reminded of what she considers a most unsports-
manly act. I never recall the incident without
smiling. I was botanizing about five miles from
our old camp on Round Lake, and had left her
with my rifle on the shore of a smaller lake
while I went to look for orchids in a tamarack

swamp several miles away. She had made a little shelter of hemlock boughs and was tucked under it reading, when this old fellow crashed through the brush on the opposite side of the lake, plunged into the water, and began swimming toward her. She had never seen so large a wild animal in the woods and her first womanly impulse was to scream, but she kept still, thinking he might turn to one side. He continued to swim straight toward her, and in her fright she aimed and shot him through the head. I heard the shot, hurried back and found her in tears. 'Take me home, oh take me home, Uncle Tom, I shot him in the water,' was all she said when I praised the shot. On our way to camp she asked to have Joe take the meat to a neighboring lumber camp and begged me not to remind her of the matter again."

Burton noted with pleasure the look of surprise on Ferris's face, as they entered the door of the "work-shop" and closed it behind them.

"You will not care to remain in here very long, as I am keeping the temperature at eighty-five and the air very moist on account of experiments I am making with certain fungi. It is really surprising how unsatisfactory the books are in regard to some of these, particularly when you consider what an important part they play in the chemistry of every-day life. I have just concluded several experiments in yeast culture that I was led to make after reading of the remarkable results obtained with the Japanese fungus, Koji, a smut grown on rice. I procured some of it after much trouble, but soon found that practically the same results could be had with the smut of corn or almost any other cereal, and I am experimenting now with common molds or fungi of various kinds. This sort of work is my hobby, but I have ridden it to advantage, for with the aid of my niece, who is particularly fond of chemistry, I have succeeded in reachiug results, the patents on which pay us a very snug income in royalties. So it is we profit by the ignorance and laziness of our fellows."

It was seven o'clock when Adam announced dinner, and here again was a surprise for Ferris, for the meal, deliciously cooked and daintily served, proved that Adam was indeed a master of his art. The old negro showed that he was also accustomed to order the household affairs, for when Burton asked if they were to have no coffee, he replied : " Your coffee will be served in your room this evening, Mr. Thomas."

"Which means, Ferris, that Adam wants to get rid of us now. Well, we will go ; he is master here."

In Burton's room they found a bright fire

that Joe had built, and above it swung a crane with a kettle of boiling water from which the coffee was soon made. Over this and their cigars the plans for the morrow were discussed. It was decided that Joe should paddle Ferris to the rapids about fifteen miles down stream; from there he could fish the river two miles to the logging road that ran to Round Lake camp. With the aid of his map Burton soon gave his guest a fair idea of the country through which he would pass, and as the camp was only a mile from the river, and the logging road very plain, he suggested that he could fish until nearly sunset and still reach the camp in time for dinner.

"Would it not be better to walk from here to the rapids?" asked Ferris, as he saw by the map that in a straight line the distance to Round Lake was much shorter than by the river.

"There are two fatal objections to that," answered Burton. "In the first place, you would disappoint Joe, who is never so happy as when showing his skill with the paddle, and in the second place, the trail, if it can be called one, is as bad as can be. It was run by the compass through swamps and windfalls and altogether without regard to the comfort of the traveller. No, you will enjoy the ride to the rapids and will find exercise enough after you reach them, in climbing over rocks and fallen logs, but you will get good fishing, I am sure."

It was agreed that as Burton could not go with Ferris because of his laboratory work, he would make the same trip on the day following.

There was a remarkable congeniality between these two, and they lingered, discussing a wide range of topics until nearly midnight. They had become friends, and as occasion offered each was told something of the other's life. Burton was forty-nine years old, although he looked much younger. He was born and had lived in the little town of Lewes on the Delaware coast until he was twenty-five, with the exception of six years spent at college and in hospital work. On the death of an uncle in Detroit, he was left a fortune ample enough to enable him to follow his studies in chemistry and medicine without practicing the latter; and, what was more to him, the management of the property took him from Lewes, where everything had gone wrong after the death of his young wife six months before. He took with him the little girl, whom he had practically although not formally adopted shortly before his wife's death, and these two lived with his invalid aunt, who, with their cheerful companionship, still lingered at the age of eighty.

"My little girl has grown to be a woman now," said Burton, with a half sigh, "and has not been in the woods for two years, during much of which time she has been abroad. We used to camp each summer at Round Lake, and Adam's cabin yonder was built as a shelter on our fishing trips. I have kept the cabin at the Lake in repair, and I assure you it will give me pleasure to see her in the woods again, for no environment fits her so well. This is her photograph," he added, after a moment's pause, handing Ferris a picture from the dressing-case.

"Why, surely," said Ferris in surprise, "I have seen this face. Has she been in Chicago?"

"Never, until a few days ago. We have always come here by boat from Detroit to Escanaba and from there by wagon into camp."

Soon after this Ferris went to his room and fell asleep trying to recall where he had seen the familiar face of the photograph. He knew no more until he was aroused by Adam's announcement of "Breakfast in half hour, sah," and found the sun streaming in at his window.

After breakfast and a cigar with Burton, Ferris and Joe started down the river in a long, narrow "dug-out" of the latter's handiwork, Ferris seated on the bottom near the bow and Joe kneeling near the stern. It was a disappointment to the Indian that Ferris took no rifle with him, as hunting was more to his liking than fishing. For several miles after leaving the cabins the river, scarcely thirty feet wide, ran in rather sluggish course between banks hedged with thickets of alders and heavy underbrush, then through tamaracks and cedars and low ground. Further on it passed the foot of a high hill, the heavy timber of which grew to the water's edge on one side, while on the other there stretched a broad meadow of rank grass, dotted with bunches of small trees and bushes on the higher points of ground.

Suddenly the boat stopped and Joe whispered :

" Keep still, deer coming in."

Ferris could see nothing in the hundred yards of open water before them, but the quick eye of the Indian was not at fault. He had seen the bending of a bush at the turn of the river such as the light breeze blowing up stream could not have made. Ferris heard the breaking of a twig, then the splash of a buck walking in the water and in a moment he appeared around the bend and in midstream before them. With head in air, he looked toward them but the Indian knelt as motionless as a statue and with his paddle held the boat as in a vise. Then as the deer turned slightly and splashed the water with his nose, still walking toward them, the canoe shot forward slightly faster than the current, twenty yards, to stop again as the deer raised his head. This was repeated and they were now within forty yards.

"Surely, he must see us," thought Ferris.

But no, he crossed the stream slowly and began to nip the tops of the tall grasses at the water's edge, while the canoe, carried by the current, was steered towards him by the motionless Indian. Then with a mighty stroke the canoe was driven forward. There was a bound, a cracking of brush, and with terrified snorts the deer was gone.

There was an expression of self-satisfaction on Joe's face as he swung the boat into midstream again, but he only said :

" Him fine buck. Too bad, no gun."

As they continued down stream Ferris leaned back upon his fish basket, and shading his eyes with his hands, watched in dreamy mood the drifting clouds and the overhanging branches of the trees along the banks. Again he recalled the photograph Burton showed him and tried to remember where he had known that face. But the canoe is now approaching the rapids and Joe tells him to get ready his rod and flies. By the time he has done this they are darting past the boulders in the narrow channel and in a moment more the boat is held against the rapid current, while Ferris has forgotten everything save the three-pound trout that is struggling for freedom at the end of his line.

This was indeed sport after his own heart, for Ferris was an enthusiastic fisherman. Never before had he met with such a perfect master of the paddle as Joe, and he would gladly have foregone his luncheon had not the Indian reminded him after the third trout had been captured, that it was "dinner time, may be." On the bank of the stream a short distance below the rapids, Joe soon built a small fire of dry sticks and birch bark. While the water was boiling for the coffee he cleaned two of the trout, and skillfully fixing them upon forked sticks broiled them above the glowing embers. The luncheon that Adam had put up for them was then spread out and found to contain a cold partridge, besides bread and butter, cookies and a glass of wild cranberry sauce. From a neighboring birch tree Joe stripped several broad sheets of bark that made excellent plates, and a luncheon that would have delighted a lover of the woods more than the most epicurean feast, was ready.

During the meal and in the half hour after, while they enjoyed their pipes, these two men, — the one a child of the forest and the other no less a lover of it,— found much to talk of, for in reality the extremes of civilization are not as

far apart as they seem. Joe's father was a full-
blooded Chippewa Indian, and his mother a Canadian French woman, but while the child of this
union had inherited a compromise complexion,
the Indian traits were strongly predominant. It
was a surprise to Ferris, however, to discover
how little Joe knew of the history of his people
and how scant was his store of tradition. With
eager interest he listened while Ferris told what
he knew of the Chippewa tribe and its Algon-
quin brethren, its battles for existence and its
wanderings, until the remnant found an abiding
place in the northern woods, where proximity to
the white man saved it from extermination by its
fiercer and more powerful foes. It is fortunate
that our Indian lore was gathered before the inter-
marrying with the whites began, for miscegena-
tion is disastrous to tradition. The story of
La Salle, as Ferris touched upon it briefly, seemed
to awaken a memory, for the Indian said :

"Him great buck. I heard old squaw tell of
him some time." But the story of his father's
people was a revelation to him.

After giving Ferris a few simple directions
how to find the Round Lake trail, some two
miles farther down, Joe pushed off his boat and
with sturdy stroke was soon above the rapids
and beyond the bend of the river. Reluctantly,
Ferris left the pool below the rapids and

began fishing down stream. As he went, the current became more swift and the banks of the stream more precipitous and difficult to fish from, but the occasional pools, although at times hard to reach, invariably repaid his efforts with one or more additions to his small fish basket until it was nearly full. At length he saw, at some distance ahead, a tall pine, the blazed trunk of which he knew marked the road he would take to camp; but between him and it was a stretch of rapids, the still water at the end of which gave promise of a happy climax to his day's sport. To reach this spot was no easy matter, for on one side the bank of the stream had caved in, dumping a mass of rocks at the edge of the pool and overturning a giant hemlock, the trunk of which had fallen across the stream while its roots still clung to the top of the bank from which it had fallen. From this tree, if he could get upon it, he could easily command the pool. Scaling the bank with some difficulty, he reached the tree and climbed over its projecting roots. Holding fast to one of these he made a cast, but the flies fell short owing to his height above the water level. Swinging his flies to the opposite side of the tree to cast again, he had begun to unreel the line, when the rotten bark on which he stood gave way and he fell upon the mass of rocks below.

CHAPTER V.

WHEN Ferris regained consciousness his first sensation was that of intense pain, and as he tried to move the suffering caused him to groan. Then he realized that his head was being supported and he heard a soft voice say :

"Poor fellow," and a moment later, "won't you try to get up? You are in the water and I am afraid you will be chilled."

Opening his eyes he met the gaze of the face that he had seen so often since Burton showed him the photograph the night before.

"This is very good of you, Miss Seaton. I must have had a bad fall. Yes, I think I can get up. Ah! that left arm is broken," he added as it hung helplessly at his side, while he allowed himself to be raised to a sitting position.

Looking down, the sight of the pool of blood where his head had struck the rocks made him feel faint again and he closed his eyes.

"Do you think you are strong enough to stand?" Madge said in persuasive tones. "Your feet are in the water and it is very cold. Let me help you and if you can walk just a little way you will find a warm fire and a comfortable bed. Now put your right arm on my shoulder and I am sure we shall get on nicely."

Ferris did as he was bidden and felt himself lifted to his feet, which were so numb that it was with difficulty he could stand. He looked up at the steep bank from which he had fallen and then at the river and said helplessly:

" There seems no alternative but swimming to get away from here."

"Oh, yes," she answered with a smile, "the water is not very deep, not above your waist and you can wade across, I am sure."

" But won't you get wet," he said in faint protest. " Surely you must be already."

"I do not mind at all. I am quite used to wet feet when I am in the woods."

Ferris tried to take a step forward without her help, but in doing so nearly fell again.

" Perhaps you had better sit here while I go to camp for help. It will take me only a few minutes."

" Pray do not go," he answered. " I am sure I can do better, at least if you will let me take your arm."

With his right arm resting on her shoulder and her left supporting much of his weight, they succeeded in reaching the opposite bank, and Ferris rested against the tall pine, the old blaze on which showed the trail to Round Lake. It was a long and weary mile for Ferris from the river to the camp, and many times he found himself involuntarily leaning heavily upon his companion's arm. But she protested that he did not allow her to help him, as an invalid should, and in her happy way encouraged him to bear up when he felt that to drag himself another step was next to a physical impossibility.

It was nearly dark when they came in sight of the tents and a loud "halloa" from Madge brought old Dan'l, who had just started the camp fire and was waiting her return before serving the dinner. With Dan'l's help Ferris was quickly relieved of his wet clothing, and after getting into a suit of Vinton's pajamas was put to bed on a cot that Dan'l brought from his own tent.

"Good liquor is a great enemy of water, we sailors think," said Dan'l, as he administered a liberal draught of what he called the best liquor this side of salt water, "though some folks don't seem to know it, judging from the way they mix 'em together," he observed, as he helped Ferris into bed.

"Can I come in now?" asked Mrs. Elting, as she heard Dan'l wish Ferris a good-night and assure him that he would feel "like a jack-tar on a shore day " in the morning. The old servant did not know it was taxing to the utmost poor Ferris's endurance to bear in silence the agony he was suffering.

"Yes, thanks," answered Ferris, and Mrs. Elting entered bringing with her such things as might be needed in dressing his wounded head and arm. Gently she removed from his head the hastily improvised bandage that Madge had placed there, a small soft handkerchief now soaked with blood from the wound it covered above the temple, and held in place by the braid torn from her skirt. Then with her scissors she cut away the hair, bathed the wound with tepid water, and drawing the edges together, applied strips of adhesive plaster with the skill of a surgeon. She realized her helplessness as she cut away the sleeve of the left arm and saw how badly it was broken; the small bone below the elbow protruding almost through the skin. This was work, indeed, for a surgeon. As she lifted the arm slightly to place it in a more natural position she heard Ferris grind his teeth together and stifle a groan. Carefully she wound a broad, soft bandage around it, not feeling quite certain that this was the right thing to do.

By the time she had finished this and had bathed his face, Ferris began to breathe heavily. The terrible shock, the loss of blood, the excru-

ciating pain, the weary walk had exhausted his
strength and for a short time, at least, he would
forget them all. But it was only for a little
while, for soon he began to move nervously and
groan in his sleep, and in less than an hour was
awake again. He did not at once recognize his
surroundings, but in a moment the thought of
what had happened and where he was came to
him. Mrs. Elting still sat by his side and his
eyes were very bright as he caught hers and with
a faint smile thanked her for her care. With
motherly gentleness she placed her hand upon
his forehead and found that he was in a fever.
She was not easily alarmed, yet she had learned
enough of illness to know that under the circumstances he might be in danger. Promising
to return in a few minutes, she went to find
Madge and determine with her aid whether it
might be possible to direct Dan'l so that he
could find Dr. Burton's cabin and get him to
Ferris without delay. Madge, who was sitting
before the smouldering camp fire, hastened to
Mrs. Elting when she saw her come from the tent.

"Is there anything I can do, Dora?" she inquired anxiously.

"No, nothing, dear, unless you can direct
Dan'l how to get to your uncle's. Mr. Ferris is
in much pain, but what worries me more is that
he is very feverish. Now you must not be

alarmed, but if you think Dan'l can find his way by the river or through the woods to Dr. Burton's cabin, I am sure that he had better start at once. You see the men will not return from Elk Lake before to-morrow noon, if so soon, and Charley may not come with them if he has to carry in the venison. Do you think Dan'l can find the way at night ? "

"No, I am certain he could not. The trail by the river is nearly twenty miles and almost impassable. The trail through the woods has not been blazed for years and I scarcely think he could follow it by daylight. No, Dan'l cannot go, but I will, and at once," she added.

"But, my dear child, that is impossible. You must not subject yourself to the danger of going alone through these woods at night. Besides, you have had a hard day already, and must be very tired. Suppose you should get lost? I could never forgive myself."

"Now, Dora dear," answered Madge, " it is good of you to think of me, but you must not worry. There is no danger in these woods at night—no animal that will not run from the human voice ; and as to my getting lost, I know every foot of the way, for these woods are like home to me. So you see there is really no cause to worry, and I will return with uncle in the morning."

In vain Mrs. Elting protested against her
going, for Madge realized the pressing need of
her uncle's presence in this extremity.

Hastily she made her preparations for the
journey, which she knew must be a hard one,
since as Burton had told Ferris, the trail was as
bad as could be and it was a long twelve miles.
She was indeed tired and the sight of food re-
pelled her, yet she ate a light dinner, knowing
that she would need strength for the journey.
In her pocket she took a few crackers, a box
of matches and a compass, and fastened to her
belt a small hunting knife and her revolver.   In
one hand she carried her tent lantern and in the
other a woolen jacket.

There is something solemn, impressive, awe-
inspiring, about a dense forest in the night.
The utter stillness, save for the uncanny sounds
of insect life that are heard at no other time, the
towering blackness of the trees, which seem so
much taller than by daylight, the queer shapes
of broken trunks and branches, the occasional
phosphorescence of a rotten stump—all con-
tribute to quicken the heart-beats even of one
who knows and loves the solitude of the woods.
And so it was that while Madge felt no fear of
anything tangible, there was that indefinite dread
or nervousness which is apt to come to even the
bravest, when subjected to the imaginary prob-

ability of meeting some mysterious foe. While she knew this trail and could have followed it easily by day, she soon realized how different and unfamiliar it was by night, and often was forced to slacken her pace and search for the obscure blazes that in many places had been obliterated by the natural growth of the trees on which they were made. Yet she knew that if the trail were lost it would be far more difficult, if not impossible in the darkness, to find her way by the compass. Each familiar landmark gladdened her heart ; even the long stretch of burnt-over windfall covered with its growth of briar bushes that scratched her hands and tore her gown, and the dense boggy tamarack swamp that in daylight she would have walked around to avoid wetting her feet, no longer daunted her. Once she sat down to rest for a little while on a fallen tree, and involuntarily the tears rolled down her face, for she knew that she had covered only half the distance and she was tired almost to exhaustion. "Courage, courage," she said to herself, and again and again silently prayed for strength to reach her destination.

At last through the woods she saw the opening where the river ran, and quickening her gait she crossed the bridge and was at the door of Burton's cabin. How her heart beat and her temples throbbed! She knocked on the door and waited a moment, but no answer. What if he had been called to Keating, she thought. Again she knocked louder than before, and this time called:

"Uncle Tom, come quickly."

In a moment she heard a door open at the other end of the cabin and saw Burton running towards her.

"What has happened, Madge dear?" he said, taking her outstretched hands as she sank to the bench beside the door. "How did you get here? You are ill, child. Were there no men in your camp that you should make this journey alone? Did Mr. Ferris know that you came alone?"

Madge had collapsed under the long strain through which she had passed and sobbed piteously as Burton questioned her rapidly.

"In a moment, Uncle dear, I will tell you all," she said, as she wiped her eyes and tried to speak. "Mr. Ferris has met with a dreadful accident. He has broken his arm and cut his head and you must go to him at once;" and again the sobs choked her voice. "Oh, do hurry and get ready, Uncle Tom, and I will tell you all afterwards."

"But, my child, I must take care of you before I can go to Ferris. Now lie down in this room," he said, as he opened the door at which she had knocked, "and I will return in a moment."

He hurried away without heeding her protest that he must not stop to think of her, and soon had Adam and Joe at work, the one building a fire in the guest room and the other filling the lantern and getting together and packing into a small bag such things as he had suitable or could improvise for the surgical work before him. During this time Adam had made for Madge a hot cup of tea and had brought a hot foot bath. When Burton returned, he found her resting quietly, the old negro hovering about her with a devotion characteristic of his race. In as few words as possible, she told how she had found Ferris after his fall, how Mrs. Elting had dressed his wound, and how after a brief sleep he had grown restless and feverish. A look of anxiety came into Burton's face, and noticing it, she said :

"Do you think Mr. Ferris's injuries may be very serious?"

"Oh, no, broken arms are not apt to be serious, but I think I may save him considerable pain, and I will lose no time in getting to him."

Bidding Madge good-bye, and promising to send Joe to fetch her by the river the next day, he returned to his laboratory for some additional drugs and then with the Indian started over the trail by which she had come.

It was midnight when they left the cabins and the clouded moon dimly lighted the woods. Joe scarcely needed the lantern that he carried to show him the trail, for he knew it by night as well as by day, and the bent grass and up-turned moss showed him as plainly the way Madge had come as if her foot-prints had been made in snow. It was with effort that Burton followed him, but he had told him to lose no time and he was obeying to the letter. It had taken Madge four hours to make the distance that they covered in three. As they approached the camp the Indian stopped an instant, for his keen ear had heard an unusual sound and he said :

"Listen, Tom, him fight."

"Go on," Burton answered sharply, hurrying rapidly forward. As they neared the tents the noises grew louder and more distinct. In his hospital work he had heard such sounds, and he quickly detected Ferris's voice speaking in the tone of intense excitement peculiar to delirium.

He paused a moment outside the tent and from a small phial carefully filled a hypodermic syringe ; then making a slight noise to attract Mrs. Elting's attention, he waited until she came out followed by Dan'l. As he entered the tent

Ferris endeavored to rise, but his strength was exhausted and he sank back upon the bed with a groan. He did not recognize Burton nor did he apparently feel the needle of the syringe as it entered his bared arm. The effect of the drug was quick and in an incoherent way he murmured:

"Bring her back again, won't you? I promise you can have what you want. Let me see her again before I go,—just a little while. She was so good to me and I did not thank her. Ah, this is cruel," and closing his eyes he breathed heavily.

Burton waited a few minutes to be sure that Ferris was under the influence of the drug and then went outside the tent.

"I think Mr. Ferris will get on comfortably," he said to Mrs. Elting whom he found anxiously waiting with Helen. "I will look after him now and you must get some rest."

"Is there nothing we can do, Doctor?" Helen asked. "I am not at all sleepy."

"No, there is nothing that will be so good for him as perfect rest. As soon as may be I will ascertain how seriously his head is injured. The broken arm is of little consequence."

Thus reassured Mrs. Elting and Helen went to their tent and Burton returned to Ferris.

"Spread your blanket in the corner, Joe, and

get some sleep," he said, as he entered the tent.
"I shall want you to go to the cabins in the
morning."

Within a few minutes the deep breathing of
the Indian told how easy he found obedience to
this order. Later Burton examined the wound
upon Ferris's head and was relieved to find that
the skull was not fractured. He knew from this
that unless the concussion had been more serious than was evidenced by the scalp wound, his
patient, with a few hours' rest, would be out of
danger, if the fever could be promptly checked.
After filling the tent stove with fresh wood, he
waited patiently for the fever to subside as the
temperature of the tent increased. In this he
was not disappointed, and within a few hours
the danger in this direction had passed.

It was broad daylight when Ferris awoke and
found Burton at his side with splints in readiness to set the broken arm. With Joe's assistance this was soon accomplished, although not
without much pain.

Having made his patient as comfortable as
possible and left him to the tender care of Mrs.
Elting, with directions as to some simple medicine to induce sleep and prevent the return of
the fever, Burton sent Joe to his cabins to bring
Madge, and then went to bed in Vinton's tent.
At intervals during the morning Ferris sought

to learn from Mrs. Elting all that had occurred
since his accident, but in obedience to Burton's
instructions, she insisted upon his silence, although she could not resist telling him that it
was Madge who had gone for Burton in the
night.

Shortly before luncheon Vinton, Whitney
and Moulton returned with Charley from Elk
Lake, bringing with them a handsome buck that
Whitney had killed the night before. Both
Vinton and Moulton had missed fair shots during the day,—a fact that in Whitney's easy
conscience justified their subsequent night-
hunting. Moulton's account of this entertained Helen as she went with him to the landing to view the head.

"When we reached the lake yesterday morning,—it seems at least a month ago,"—he
said, "Charley posted us at different places
while he made a wide detour through the woods.
My position was on a little point that com-
manded a bay scarcely a hundred yards across
and which for a half hour I watched so intently
that I am sure, were I an artist, I could repro-
duce its every tree, and twig and leaf. Then I
remembered an unfinished story in my pocket
and concluded that I could quite as well relieve
my eyes and brain with that. I had just lighted
a cigar and was beginning to feel that still

hunting wasn't so bad after all, when I heard a
crash in the brush near me and, looking up, saw
a deer not fifty yards away.   Considering the
fact that the deer is a most timid and harmless
creature, it is marvellous what a commotion
akin to terror the sudden appearance of one can
arouse.   My heart beat like a trip-hammer and
the perspiration stood in beads upon my forehead.   I dropped my book and, in a spirit of
self defense, I think, reached for my rifle,
which stood against an adjacent stump.   This
attracted the animal's attention and with a snort,
indicative of disgust, no doubt, he turned and
started for the timber.   As he did so, I fired,
but of course the bullet went wide of the mark,
for my hand was trembling like an aspen.   Your
brother was unkind enough to diagnose my case
as one of 'buck fever.'   An hour later Vinton
missed a shot and I felt in a measure consoled.

    "Of course our explanations were interesting,
but they did not help out the larder, and immediately after supper we decided to try our luck
by night.   Charley had resurrected an ancient
dug-out, and in the bow of this he set up a staff
to which we fastened the head-light.   Immediately behind this Merrick knelt with his rifle in
front of him, while I sat in the waist and Charley
paddled in the stern.   The night was very cold,
and as our boat crept along the edge of the shore

the mist rising from the water seemed to pene-
trate my very bones, notwithstanding I had on
numerous flannel shirts, a top coat and a blanket.
I think I would have wrapped the shelter tent
about me also if Vinton had not been beneath
it. But it was exciting, I assure you. I sat
there in a tremor of expectation and cold, straining my eyes on each point of the shore as Merrick turned his light upon it. The stillness was
deathlike except for the occasional thumping of
beetles against the lamp, from which they seemed
to take refuge on my face, and the jumping of
fish as we broke their surface slumbers. Until
you have tried it, you can have no idea how
startling it is at night to have some leviathan of
the deep, or what seems like one, dart suddenly
from beneath the bow of your boat. We had
nearly completed the circuit of the lake, gliding
noiselessly in and out its little bays where the
rushes would permit, when suddenly I felt the
boat shake. This apparently excited a new set
of nerves, and I was tempted to jump out and
swim ashore, when I remembered that it was
Charley's signal that a deer was at hand. At
first I could see nothing; but, as Merrick swung
his light towards the shore, two eyes like balls of
fire loomed against the black background of the
trees. Slowly the boat crept toward them, and
at a second signal from Charley, Merrick raised

his rifle and fired.   Our boat darted forward, and in a moment we were in shallow water, and Merrick and Charley gave the *coup de grace* to this monarch of the forest."

In the afternoon Vinton and Moulton were allowed to see Ferris, and later Madge came, bringing with Adam's compliments, a brace of partridges for his dinner. On the following morning Burton started for his cabins, having first exacted from his patient a promise that he would remain in bed until his return the next day.

CHAPTER VI.

FERRIS had not been ill since his childhood, and after three days' confinement in bed, he welcomed the morning on which Burton was to return and let him up. Every one had been very attentive to him and contributed in every possible way toward his entertainment, but he felt sorely tempted, as his strength returned, to break the promise which, in his weak condition, seemed so easy to make.

Through the open flaps of his tent he could see different members of the party preparing for the diversions of the day. Vinton had set his heart on getting a buck, and not discouraged by the fact that he had missed two the day before, had taken an early breakfast and gone with the Indian for an all-day tramp. Whitney had also gone early to catch the morning flight of some duck he had seen the day before in a neighboring lake, and Madge was preparing to meet him there and show him the whereabouts of a covey of partridges before returning for luncheon. Helen and Moulton had spent an hour in planning just where they should go. Moulton had suggested and argued stoutly in favor of a bear hunt and other equally absurd plans as a way of consuming the morning hours, and had varied his argument with a discussion of a wide range of topics, from the latest light opera, snatches of which he illustrated on the banjo, and with which he was entirely familiar, to the habits of the black bear and the best methods of hunting him, about which he knew nothing.

The Gordian knot of this embarrassing question was at last cut by old Dan'l, who had been taking in the conversation, as he busied himself about his culinary duties.

"Mr. Moulton, sor, if it would not interfere with your slaughtering of the bear, ye might take the small basket and pick some blueberries, and I'll give ye some foin pies, sor, for dinner."

"That is a capital suggestion, Dan'l; there is no place where one is so apt to meet the black bear as in a blueberry patch. I think I might quote even Audubon as an authority for that, Miss Seaton."

And so they started around the edge of the lake, Moulton carrying the basket and Helen a light novel. In a few minutes Moulton returned.

"What's the matter, Tom?" Ferris asked as

he entered the tent; "I thought you and Miss Whitney had gone on a bear hunt."

"Well, we did start; but she has just called my attention to the fact that I forgot my rifle, and I have come back for it."

He took the rifle from the rack and was leaving the tent, when Ferris called: "Hold on, Tom, won't you need some cartridges? Hunters frequently do."

"Don't be funny, Bob," he answered, as he snatched up a cartridge belt and hurried away.

In a little while Mrs. Elting came to Ferris's tent and began reading aloud; but he thought little of the story, for he was watching Madge as she wiped out her shotgun and filled the pockets of her short coat with shells. He smiled as he saw her look through the polished barrels and with the affectionate care of a veteran sportsman run her white hand over the brown metal from breech to muzzle.

"Has our invalid any choice of game?" she asked lightly as she stood a moment in front of the tent before going.

"Well, Miss Aladdin, since you suggest it, I think my dainty appetite craves the luscious breast of the dusky mallard," Ferris answered in the same vein.

With an oriental courtesy she disappeared, and for a few minutes later he could see her kneeling straight as an Indian, as she paddled her canoe across the lake.

Toward noon Burton appeared, closely followed by Joe, each bearing on his back a weighty pack, sustained by a broad strap extending around the shoulders and chest. Relieving himself of his burden and directing Joe where to put up the "A" tent which it contained, Burton entered Ferris's tent and examined his head and arm.

"I think the chances are largely in favor of your recovery," he said with a smile as he finished.

"Not if I have to stay in bed any longer," answered Ferris rather impatiently.

"Tut, tut, man, a fracture of the radius should be good for at least ten days' attendance, from a professional standpoint. Would you have me belittle the science of surgery by permitting you to get up at the end of the fourth day? However, as I have no license to practice in this state and there are no fellow-practitioners in the immediate neighborhood to criticise my treatment of your case, I will risk the charge of malpractice and breach of professional ethics, and allow you to dress."

In a short time, with the assistance of Burton, he got into his clothes, and the two walked along the shore together. During his absence Burton had gone to Keating, and he reported to Ferris that the little town had returned to its normal condition of quiet industry.

"I had the pleasure of seeing the sheriff of the county escort Tim Finney and his right-hand man, Dutchy, to the train in irons, and a more villainous looking couple I never saw."

"I am gratified to know that this county has a sheriff. We certainly had no occasion to suspect the existence of such an official during the strike."

"Oh ! it was not for any part he played in the strike that Tim was arrested. Our sheriff is far too good a politician for that. It was discovered that it was Finney and his man who robbed the superintendent of the Denton mines last week, and such a crime our sheriff regards as far more heinous than the attempt to wreck the plant of a corporation, even if the latter offense might endanger the lives of its hirelings. I saw your mail-boy also, and found him as lively as a cricket. As I was leaving the town, a little woman stopped me and said that my patient, Jack Turnley, was much better, and with many blushes added that they 'would be married next month,' if Jack got back his job."

"He shall have it, then," said Ferris, after a moment's pause, during which he saw a small boat put out from the opposite shore and recognized the trim figure of its occupant.

"Is not that rather a treasonable remark from such a confirmed bachelor?"

"Perhaps," answered Ferris; "but you see I have not altogether recovered yet."

Continuing their walk a half mile further, they came to a deserted logging road that ran to the lake where it was overgrown with berry bushes. Against the stump of an old pine tree that stood by its side, leaned a rifle, with a cartridge belt hanging across the muzzle.

"This is Tom Moulton's idea of hunting," said Ferris, as they turned into the wood.

"Or this," said Burton, with a smile, pointing farther up the road where it ran into the heavy timber and was free from underbrush.

There on the trunk of a tree that had fallen across the road, Helen was sitting, reading aloud from her novel, while at her feet Moulton was stretched on the ground with his chin resting on his hands and looking very intently at the fair reader.

"Do you suppose that man has any idea that it is nearly time for luncheon?" asked Burton.

"A week ago I should have said 'yes,' for Tom has usually a vigorous and exacting appetite; but I am beginning to doubt whether such material things seem so important to him now as they did."

As they drew near, Helen heard them, and

looked up from her book. Seeing Ferris and Burton, she came toward them.

"I am delighted to see you out again, Mr. Ferris, and to have you with us, Doctor," she said. "Have you any cure for laziness?" she added, as Moulton slowly rose and shook hands with Burton.

"If it is uncomplicated with other diseases, there is nothing better than absolute rest."

"Thanks, Doctor, that is a most excellent prescription, and one I can easily fill here."

"But not just now, Tom," said Ferris, "for you must go back to luncheon, and must lug the rifle and cartridge belt, if bruin has not carried them off."

"Why, really, I had no idea it was so late," said Moulton, looking at his watch. "How time does slip away here."

"When one is hunting," added Ferris. "Where is your rifle?"

"Let me see, I think I stood it against a tree, when we went to pick berries. Where did we put it, Miss Whitney?"

"Never mind, Tom, we will get it as we go along."

When they reached camp, they found that Madge had already returned. On the front pole of the men's tent hung a single duck. Ferris did not notice it until he heard Burton exclaim:

"Hello! This is a beauty. And a genuine dusky old drake," he added, as he examined the black bill and feet of the mallard.

"Are you enough of a taxidermist, Doctor, to save that skin for me?" asked Ferris, as he saw what a fine specimen it was. "I should like to have it mounted."

"O, yes, that is very simple," answered Burton, "but you should have the mate to go with it."

Just then Madge appeared from her tent, where she had changed her shooting coat for a blue jacket.

"I am glad you were not with me, Uncle Tom, when I made that shot. You would have been ashamed of your pupil. I had a beautiful chance for a right and left in the little lake beyond the river. With the right, I got this old fellow, and I thought at first I had his mate with the left, but she rose over the timber and disappeared in the direction of Bass Lake, where Mr. Whitney is shooting. What an enthusiast he is! I left him munching crackers, as he preferred to miss luncheon and wait for the evening flight. He has had little chance to shoot ducks before, and seems fascinated with it."

"I am not surprised," said Ferris, "for there is no sport to equal it. Until three years ago I had never shot a duck, although I had hunted a great deal for larger game. There is a variety and excitement about it that one cannot find in field shooting, or in the mountains."

"Miss Seaton will agree with you, I am sure," said Burton. "It is one of the points on which she and I differ, as I prefer the rifle to the shotgun always."

"He says it is more exact," said Madge. "Uncle is nothing, if not exact. He always insists on eliminating the element of chance, while, for my part, I depend upon it largely. It has saved the reputation of many a poor sportsman like myself."

Soon after luncheon, Helen joined Mrs. Elting in the tent. Burton, in his methodical way, went to bed, to catch up his lost sleep, and Moulton wandered down the lake shore for a swim. Ferris was enjoying the soft September air in an easy camp chair on the edge of the bluff, watching the shadows on the still water of the slowly drifting clouds, when Madge appeared with a novel under her arm.

"You are feeling quite well again, are you not, Mr. Ferris?"

"If I say yes, will it deprive me of sharing your book with you?" he answered.

"If you knew what it is, I fear you would prefer to escape it. It is a light novel, but full of excitement, I am told. I have not yet begun it."

"What else should novels be?" said Ferris. "For my part, it is the kind I most thoroughly enjoy. I think the first object of a novel should be to entertain the reader. If incidentally it can administer a modest amount of instruction sufficiently disguised, that is not bad ; but unfortunately, so many of the novelists of to-day seem to confound their mission with that of the sociologist, the clergyman, the moralist, and the general pedagogue, that the leaven of excitement is not sufficient to raise the mass of general dullness. Now that I have given my views so frankly, may I ask the name of your book?"

"It is 'That Lass o' Lowrie's,' by Frances Hodgson Burnett. It was recommended to me by Mr. Kennedy, who claims the writer as a country-woman of his."

"That is true in part only," answered Ferris, "as she came to this country when a mere child. I have been waiting for a chance to read the book, and am delighted that you should have it. Won't you sit here and read?"

"No, thank you, I will take the hammock."

Arranging the pillows so that she could get a view of the lake, Madge began to read. Her voice was low and musical, and she read with distinctness, for she had long been accustomed to reading aloud to old Miss Burton, whose eye-

sight was very poor.   It was a novel sensation
for Ferris to be read to thus, and altogether delightful.   He closed his eyes as he listened in
dreamy mood, with one hand above his head;
and while he kept the thread of the story, he
time and again found his thoughts wandering
off on little castle-building excursions quite un-
like anything he had known before.   Yet he always "heard the music, though he missed the
tune."

Suddenly Madge ceased reading, and glanc-
ing up, Ferris saw tears in her eyes.   She was
looking out over the lake, and the book lay
closed on her lap.

"What is it?" he asked gently.

"Nothing, absolutely nothing but my own
silly imagination," she answered.   "Yet, while
I read, this is not fiction for me; it is reality.
For the time, I know that woman's heart,—we
are one.   But it has passed now," she added,
swinging herself lightly from the hammock.
"Let me show you that I am made of sterner
stuff; I will take you around the lake in my
canoe, that you may see how beautiful it is."

In a few minutes the little boat started, with
Ferris seated on a low thwart, facing the bow,
and Madge kneeling behind him, in her favorite
position when paddling.   The boat glided
steadily under her easy strokes and soon swung

toward the shore. As they moved through the tall rushes that fringed the beach, Ferris thought they would land, but beyond these they came to a little pond of clear water on one side of which was the outlet of the lake.

"Are you fond of bass fishing, Mr. Ferris?" asked Madge, as she checked the boat with her paddle.

"Very," he answered; "but they will not rise to the fly so early in the season as this, I imagine."

"Perhaps not, but I remember when I was here last, that at this outlet they rose even earlier. Give me the rod and fly book, and let us see if the same eccentric school of fish is still here."

She jointed the rod, and running the line through the rings, attached a leader with three tempting flies of gaudy color.

"That is the same cast I used the last time I was here. Will you try it? I will help you if you get a strike."

"No, let me watch you."

Away flew the flies toward the further side of the pond, and slowly Madge wound in the line. As it neared the boat, there was a splash, but the fish was wary. Again the flies dropped lightly, farther out, and scarcely had they touched the water when they disappeared, and the slender rod bent under the strain of the line as it was drawn rapidly from the reel.

"Bravo! You have him," exclaimed Ferris.

"Not yet," she answered, watching the line intently, "see him jump." As she spoke, the fish darted toward the boat and rose clear two feet above the water, shaking the hook from his mouth.

"He deserves his freedom, for that was cleverly done," exclaimed Madge, slowly winding in the line.

"Let us try once more, and I think I can show you how we may foil him if he attempt the same trick again," answered Ferris; and taking the rod, he explained how the line should be kept taut when the fish leaped from the water. The next casts were more successful, and soon four fine bass were captured.

"You see we can accomplish more together than alone," said Ferris, as Madge turned the boat toward the lake; and as he spoke he realized, that without meaning to do so, he was giving voice to another thought than that to which his words applied.

"Yes, while you are disabled," she answered, and as his eyes met hers, he saw that she, at least, was thinking only of the fishing.

The sun was setting behind the woods as they neared the camp, and the little white tents stood out in bold relief against the green and brown background of the trees. A thread of smoke was rising from the cook's tent, and they could see old Dan'l moving busily about preparing the evening meal.

"Captain Vinton has returned," said Madge, quickening her stroke. "And he has been successful, too. Do you see the deer hanging from the fallen tree on the shore beyond the camp? How pleased he must be."

As their boat touched the landing, Vinton came from his tent, and hurrying toward them, called to Ferris:

"You can never jeer at my marksmanship again, my boy, for I got that fine old buck with a single shot, and he was on the jump. Isn't he a beauty?"

"Truly, Uncle Phil, and in the blue coat too. I congratulate you. Did Joe have a rifle also?"

"Come now, Bob, I must resent that insinuation. I suppose that when I have the head mounted, I must accompany it with Joe's affidavit that I was the sole slayer. Miss Seaton, I shall present it to you, if you can find a place for it among your many trophies."

"Indeed, it shall have the place of honor, and I will not require the affidavit," answered Madge, looking with mock severity at Ferris.

"But you must confess, Uncle Phil, that your

past record does not justify any great degree of
confidence in your skill with the rifle."

"Never mind that. I am just beginning; a
trifle late in life, I confess; but I have felt
younger — yes, and happier — since I came here
than in many years. And," he added, with a
touch of feeling in the tone, "I have this little
woman to thank, in great part, for it."

Ferris noticed a slight tinge of color come
into Madge's cheek, and saw the pleasure Vinton's words gave her.

While confined to his tent, he had observed
that she and Vinton were much together and
enjoyed each other thoroughly, yet it had never
occurred to him to question that the feeling between them might be other than one of good
comradeship, for Vinton was more than twenty
years her senior and seemed even older. Now it
came to him that their fondness for each other
might mean something more than good-fellowship, and that to Vinton, perhaps, had at last
come that feeling with which even the oldest
hearts grow young; and although he loved him
above all other men, the thought was uncomfortable, and he tried to put it away.

While they were admiring Vinton's buck,
Helen and Moulton came from the woods and
joined them.

"Perhaps you might have been as lucky, if

you had been more energetic and gone hunting with Captain Vinton this morning," she said to Moulton.

"No doubt of it," he answered; "but you know the rule of our camp is, we shall shoot only what meat we can use, and Captain Vinton had his heart set on getting a buck, while I am not so enthusiastic a hunter. You should commend my unselfishness. I am very well satisfied with my day—thanks to you."

It had not occurred to Ferris to speak to Madge of the pleasure she had given him, and yet he was conscious it had been the happiest day he had ever known. He was annoyed at himself to think he had not had the thoughtfulness to express his appreciation, and he was about to do so when she called his attention to Whitney, who was coming along the shore with gun in hand and a bunch of ducks swung over his shoulder.

"Here comes our enthusiast. Let us see what he has," she said, going toward him.

"Hello! Bob, glad to see you up," said Whitney, as they joined him. "What a day I've had. Why didn't you tell me what duck shooting is? I feel as if I had wasted about ten years of my life. Jove! but I'm hungry."

Ferris examined the ducks as Whitney trudged

along beneath their weight — for there were twenty in all.

"Are they all wood duck?" he asked.

"No, there are several teal, a merganser, and one that I do not know at all, nor can I claim the credit of having shot it. It simply died a natural death, and selected my vicinity for that purpose. When Miss Seaton joined me this morning I had shot only four ; I couldn't get into the line of flight ; I had no decoys, but with four sharp sticks she set up my dead birds so that they made the best of decoys. Commend me to fair woman for methods of deception."

At the landing Whitney counted over and laid out his birds with the enthusiasm of a juvenile sportsman.

"That is my unknown ugly duckling," he said. "What is it?" "A dusky mallard," answered Ferris, "and it probably died of a broken heart, as its companion was shot by Miss Seaton this morning. Give it to me, Merrick, and I shall have them mounted, that they may be re-united."

"I disclaim the ownership of a bird slain in such a peculiarly feminine way," said Whitney. "But take it, Bob ; it may remind you what a dangerous person Miss Seaton is."

"Or, better still, that our game is not always

lost when we think it is," added Burton, as he joined them with Mrs. Elting.

Ferris colored slightly as he took the bird, and said :

"At any rate, it will remind me of a most enjoyable day."

It seemed to him a silly little speech, and so conventional, and he wished that he had kept silent. It had indeed been the happiest day he had ever known, and while he did not mean to tell Madge this, he had hoped to express to her in a less commonplace way his enjoyment.

At dinner he sat opposite Madge, whose seat was between Vinton and Burton. She was in high spirits, as indeed were all the others except himself. For some unaccountable reason he was beginning to feel depressed, and although he endeavored to join in the general good-fellowship, he realized that he was failing hopelessly, and finally abandoned the attempt. Again and again he found the thought recurring that possibly Vinton and Madge loved each other, for they seemed so entirely happy together, and her freedom with him was scarcely less than with her uncle.

"Can you imagine anything more delightful than this ?" he heard her say to Vinton. "How beautiful this place is. I did not know I loved it so. See the exquisite cloud-tints; and the pines on the other shore, mirrored as sharply in the water as they appear against the horizon. Ah, there is no place like the woods! "

" True, indeed," answered Vinton. "A genuine love of the woods is never unrequited. We may tire of city life, of travel, of too many people, or too few, but when we come back to the woods, we can shed our cares as the trees their withered leaves, and take into our lives a new happiness. But where is your enthusiasm, Bob?" he asked, speaking to Ferris. "I never knew you silent before when the praises of the woods were being sung."

" Even the woods can't make one unmindful of a broken arm, Uncle, particularly if its owner must do justice to so good a dinner single-handed," answered Ferris, rather wearily.

"I am afraid, Madge dear, that you have not proved a very good nurse to-day. You have allowed your invalid to overtax his strength," said Mrs. Elting.

"I am very sorry," answered Madge. "I should have been more thoughtful."

" Not at all, Miss Seaton, I am not tired, and my arm is simply inconvenient, not painful."

But it was plain to Ferris that the others thought him tired, and he was glad of the excuse to go to his tent soon after the dinner. That he was miserable there was no doubt, although he could not account for it. He lay on the bed with the blankets drawn over him, for the air was chilly, and through the open front of his tent watched the others gathered round the roaring camp-fire that blazed and crackled as it threw its myriad stars high into the leafy shadows.

Helen and Moulton were sitting on a low bench facing him. That they were very happy was beyond question ; and while he could not hear their conversation, he could catch occasional snatches of song and the strum of the banjo, as Moulton alone, or with Helen, sang some light tune.

Vinton and Madge were nearer to him, with their backs toward his tent, but he could see that they were absorbed in each other and rarely spoke to the others. Burton was evidently entertaining Mrs. Elting with an account of the labor troubles, for the little woman's face was brilliant with excitement and interest. Whitney was interviewing Joe at the cook's tent about the local geography and the best places for finding game, for they were to hunt together in the morning.

Watching the others thus was diverting for a time, but Ferris found himself growing more and more restless and uncomfortable. "Bob Ferris, you are a fool," he said at length, in a half undertone, and throwing off the blankets, got up and lowered the flaps of his tent.   In a moment Burton appeared, and after helping him to get ready for bed, examined his broken arm.

"I hope you find my arm doing well, Doctor, for I think I shall start for the town to-morrow.   May I break the journey at your cabin ?"

"Nonsense, man, you can't go to-morrow. You'll not be in shape to travel for several days at least.   Besides, you've had no chance for pleasure yet, and are just getting to a point where you can enjoy yourself.   You should spend a week here, and you will find it an immense help to you."

"Nevertheless, I think I shall make the start, if you will let me take your Indian to-morrow. I am good for so short a journey, I am sure."

"If you are determined, I shall go with you myself, although I had intended to remain several days longer.   Seriously, Ferris, you should not go before Monday, and I trust you will wait and go with me."

Ferris hesitated a moment, and said : "If you insist upon it I will wait."

"I must insist," answered Burton ;   "there would certainly be a risk in your going sooner."

As Burton was leaving the tent, Ferris said : "Please do not mention my going ; I told Captain Vinton yesterday I would probably remain a week longer.''

Soon after this the party about the camp-fire broke up, and Moulton, humming a lively air, came into the tent.   Ferris was in no mood to talk, and closing his eyes, pretended to sleep.

CHAPTER VII.

THE world was moving happily with Tom Moulton, and he appreciated the fact. He had made the discovery that he was very much in love with Helen, but it did not disturb him seriously. "Be philosophical, Thomas," he said to himself, "she can't possibly get away from you for three weeks yet; therefore, enjoy so much of life, at least, and don't precipitate the possibility of misery by a proposal. If she cares for you, she won't change, and if she doesn't, you will discover it soon enough. Don't inflict too much of your society upon her. Give her a chance to realize by your absence what a good comrade you are."

It was in keeping with this plan that he accepted Whitney's invitation to join him and Joe in an effort to find a bear on the following morning.

At break of day Joe slipped into the tent and waked them.

"Get up, Tom," said Whitney softly, that he might not disturb Ferris. "We must start in a half hour."

"Go ahead without me, Merrick," he answered sleepily. "I shouldn't know a bear from a Newfoundland dog at this hour. Besides, it's beastly cold."

"You'll feel all right when you have had a cup of hot coffee. Come, get up."

"What a fool I was to join such an enterprise. I never did care for bear hunting. Don't you think it would be much more sensible to wait about three hours, get a decent bath and breakfast, and then start out? Bears have to stay some place. They don't disappear from the face of the earth; so why can't we find them later as well as now?"

"Nonsense," answered Whitney; "get up, and I will tell you all about it as we go along."

Moulton did get up, but he dressed so leisurely that Joe came to the tent several times to urge greater haste. His plan, as outlined to Whitney the night before, was to visit a deserted logging camp, some three miles away, where he had a few days before noticed that a bear had been digging about the swill spout. Failing to find one there, they were to follow down the river to a swamp, through which they would hunt, and return by way of the old camp about sunset.

Dan'l had prepared their lunches the night before, and after a light breakfast they started across the lake over which the fog was hanging so dense as to obscure the opposite shore.

"Merrick," said Moulton, as he settled himself in the bow of the boat, "there is something radically wrong about a man who can deliberately do this sort of thing. Have you committed any especially heinous crime, that you should select this particular mode of penance?"

"Wait until you catch a glimpse of bruin, and you will forget that you missed your morning nap," answered Whitney. "Think of the halo of glory that will surround you when you tell at the Club how you slipped out, careless like, before breakfast and shot your first bear."

"All right," said Moulton, as he lit his pipe; "but if that bear does not materialize, I shall consider that I owe you a lasting grudge."

The eastern sky was growing crimson with the rising sun as they drew their boat on the beach and hurried through the woods. As they neared the old camp, Joe motioned to them to stop, while he went cautiously ahead; for notwithstanding his care in avoiding twigs and bushes, Moulton made much noise as he walked. In a few moments the Indian returned. "Too bad," he said, "we too late. Bear gone. Big one and cub."

"Did you notice any signs, Joe, that would

indicate whether they would return soon, or had moved into the next county?" said Moulton.

"Them go to swamp. We get 'em there or here to-night, maybe," replied the Indian.

"Ye gods! Must we live on the pleasures of hope all day?"

. As they passed near the camp, Joe pointed out where the bear had torn up the earth near the swill spout, and the fresh tracks of the great claws in the soft dirt aroused a degree of enthusiasm even in Moulton. But this ebbed after tramping an hour or so along the river bank, and when the edge of the swamp was reached, he decided to let Whitney and Joe continue the hunt, while he waited for them either there or at the deserted camp.

"You can't miss getting to the old camp from here, but don't leave it until we come, for you could never find your way from there to the lake," said Whitney, as he started with Joe into the swamp.

Moulton watched them clambering through underbrush and over fallen timber until they were out of sight. Then looking at his watch, he discovered that it was only nine o'clock. He shook the watch and put it to his ear. "Heavens!" he said half aloud, as he found the watch running, "can it be possible? I thought it was at least noon. How am I to kill the time till five,—eight hours ! Tom Moulton, you 're an idiot."

Seating himself on a fallen tree trunk, he slowly filled his pipe and began planning how he might best divide the time until his fellow hunters returned. Through the green of the timber, between where he sat and the river, he saw a bright patch of crimson, a single maple that had already taken on the glory of the autumn coloring. He rested his gun against the log. He knew some one who might, he thought, be pleased with a bunch of those bright leaves, and in a little while he had gathered them and added a few ferns and an orchid that he found on the edge of the swamp. Taking his rifle again, he followed lazily up the river, startling a covey of spruce grouse, which, with a succession of sudden whirrs, rose from almost beneath his feet and perched in the pines in front of him. "Now," thought Moulton, "if I were as expert as Miss Seaton, I might skill-fully decapitate a few of them and take their unscathed bodies back to camp. As it is, I should probably miss altogether, or tear the bodies to atoms, leaving the heads as sad re-minders of my bad marksmanship. I will ignore such small game. I am bear hunting."

It was nearly noon when he reached the cabin. Finding a chair of boards rudely but comfortably made, with an inclined back, such as are common to all lumber camps, he stretched himself on it, and from his shell-bag took such luncheon as he wanted. But he was not very hungry, and the meal was soon finished. He had never seen a lumber camp before, and he began now to investigate with interest the remains of this one. Along each side of the room, the log walls of which were chinked with moss and clay, extended two rows of bunks partially filled with hay and withered hemlock boughs—rough beds, but welcome enough to men who have toiled twelve hours, in snow to the waist, with the thermometer below zero. At one corner of the cabin was a little room partitioned off for the camp foreman, the walls of which were decorated with black and colored prints of prize-fighters, of actresses in various stages of nudity, and with thrilling pictures from the " Police News" and like periodicals that infest the logging camp. A huge rusty stove, with its pipe projecting through the roof, stood in the middle of the room, and above it were stretched wires on which the men, in winter, were accustomed to dry, or at least to warm, at night the reeking clothing that must be worn on the morrow. On shelves above the bunks were numerous bottles, empty, or containing the remnants of some patent medicines that only the stomach of a woodsman could withstand.

"What a commentary on the endurance of human nature," said Moulton, as he drew his chair to the open doorway of the cabin to escape the odor of uncleanliness that pervaded the place. "It seems like a great conspiracy to ruin men's bodies and souls alike."

In one of the bunks he had found the fragments of a trashy novel, and after attempting for an hour to divert himself with it, he threw it aside, and drawing his cap down over his eyes was soon asleep.

It was half-past four when he awoke and looked at his watch. As the air was chill, he decided to walk along the river and meet Whitney and Joe on their return. As he started from the cabin, he heard a noise like the grunt of a hog, and saw over the top of an old pork barrel that was half buried in the berry bushes at one side of the cabin a shaggy black object partly within the barrel. He did not recognize the creature at once and started toward it to get a better view; but scarcely had he made ten steps when the head and shoulders of a bear appeared above the barrel. In truth, the sight was not a pleasant one, for Moulton knew that he was no rifle shot, and at such close quarters he realized that the bear could catch him if disposed to do so. But bruin evidently had no such intention, and leisurely turning tail began to amble slowly across the clearing toward the woods. At the same time Moulton's courage returned, and as the bear scrambled over a fallen log on the edge of the timber, he aimed and fired. As the smoke of the powder cleared away, he paused an instant to see if the beast had turned upon him, but finding that the game had disappeared, he rested his rifle upon the ground and said, as many better sportsmen had said before him :

"What a fool I was to let him get away."

He was very courageous now, and, taking his weapon, hurried toward the point where the bear was last seen, but he was somewhat uncertain as to the exact spot, and was walking in the direction of the river when he noticed patches of fresh blood upon the ferns and bushes. From this he knew that his shot had taken effect, and he proceeded to follow the trail of the wounded animal as rapidly as possible. Through underbrush, over fallen logs, on high ground and bog, he hurried in his excitement, regardless alike of time and direction, now losing the trail and again stopping for an instant to note the pools of blood where the bear had evidently paused or had ejected a quantity from his mouth.

How long this chase continued he had no idea, but the end was unexpected. As he pressed hastily through a clump of dense bushes, with his head lowered and his arms raised in front to

protect his eyes, his foot encountered an obstruc-
tion, and he fell prone upon it. It was the bear,
and fortunately for Moulton it was dead. With
a yell that would have done credit to a Co-
manche Indian, he scrambled off the body and
through the brush, leaving his cap and rifle and
tearing his hands and clothing in his mad flight.
Nor did he pause until, out of breath, he found
himself on the swampy edge of a small lake.
When he realized that the bear must be dead, he
slowly and carefully retraced his steps to the
clump of bushes where the body lay, and peer-
ing cautiously in, saw on it his cap and rifle as
he had dropped them. He was too much exhausted to give voice to his triumphant feeling,
but after making sure that the breath of life had
indeed departed from the great body, he decided
to return to the cabin for Whitney and Joe to
assist in getting his game into camp, and, that
he might make better speed, left his rifle on the
bear. As he tried to follow the blood-marked
trail over which he had come, he realized for the
first time that it was growing late. Again and
again he was forced to examine the ground
closely, and soon was compelled to abandon the
attempt altogether, so rapidly did the darkness
come on. But he believed that he could find
his way to the old cabin, and struck out briskly
in what he conceived to be the most direct line

for it, nor did he discover his error until after a rapid walk of a half hour he found himself on low ground, such as he had not passed over except by the little lake near which the bear had fallen.

Any one who has had the experience of being lost in such woods can appreciate Moulton's feelings as he realized his predicament. But he did the wisest thing under the circumstances ; he stopped, and to steady his nerves slowly filled his pipe and began to smoke.

It was after five o'clock when Whitney and the Indian reached the old logging camp, for their tramp through the swamp had taken longer than they had intended. They had found no game, and as Whitney was tired and hungry they decided to pick up Moulton and hurry on to camp. When they discovered that the cabin was deserted they concluded he had gone back to the lake. From time to time as they walked rapidly along, Joe stopped to examine the trail.

"Big fellow don't come this way," he said at length. "He lost, maybe."

"Nonsense, Joe," replied Whitney. "He probably made a bee-line for our camp as soon as he left us this morning."

But at the shore of the lake they found their boat as they had left it, and no new foot-prints to indicate that Moulton had been there.

"Perhaps he has gone back around the shore. We will paddle over and see," said Whitney; and beginning to feel some uneasiness as to Moulton's whereabouts, he took a paddle and helped to drive the canoe toward camp as quickly as possible.

The camp-fire was burning brightly, and through the open end of the dining tent they could see their party at dinner. But Moulton was not in his place.

As their boat touched the landing, Whitney hurried to the camp and asked : " Where's Moulton? "

" He has not returned," answered Burton. " He was with you, we thought."

Whitney told briefly how Moulton had left them in the morning, and how, not finding him, they concluded he had gone back to camp.

"How could you come back without him, Merrick?" said Helen, with mingled annoyance and anxiety in her tone. "You know he is utterly ignorant of the woods, and is just as apt to be going away from camp as toward it."

" Now, Helen dear, don't be unreasonable. I did not lose him, but I shall certainly make every effort to find him, if you will let me have some dinner first."

"You need not feel anxiety, Miss Whitney," said Burton. "There is no danger from wild animals in these woods, and he cannot be lost very long. If he travels away from our lake, he will soon reach the river, and, following it in either direction for ten miles, he will find a well-beaten road along which he can get to civilization. The worst that can happen is that he may pass a very uncomfortable night if we do not overtake him, and may feel somewhat hungry before he encounters anything more nourishing than blueberries. But we will go in search of him without delay, and I think we shall find him without trouble. Get your dinner, Joe, as quickly as possible, and have Charley get his. Madge, will you look after the lanterns?"

It required but little time for Whitney and the Indian to finish their meal. Ferris insisted on joining the searching party, and Burton consented upon condition that he would restrict his walk to the river along the trail over which he had come first to the camp. Vinton was instructed to go toward the river at a short distance from the same trail; Whitney and Joe were to go directly to the old logging camp and look for traces of Moulton there, while Burton and Charley were to take a more southerly course, as they had done but little tramping during the day.

"I will go in your boat across the lake, Uncle Tom," said Madge, as Burton was about to

start. " I am not at all tired, and I can cover
the ground between you and Mr. Whitney."

"I think you would be of more service if you
should go with Mr. Ferris," replied Burton.
"He cannot shoot, and we shall need to fire a
signal in case of success — three shots in quick
succession."

"As you think best," she answered. " Will
you take the lantern, Mr. Ferris, while I get my
rifle?"

Helen followed her to the tent. " Madge
dear, do you think anything has happened to
him?" she said, her voice trembling as she
spoke.

"Do not worry, dearie ; I am sure not. I
know we shall find him soon," and looking into
Helen's eyes, she read her secret, and kissed her
as she hurried away to join Ferris.

It had been a very quiet day for Ferris, and
for the most part, a very uncomfortable one. He
had not fallen asleep until nearly daylight, and
did not awaken until after the others had breakfasted, and, with the exception of Burton and
Mrs. Elting, had deserted the camp. Vinton
and Madge had gone after partridges, and
across the lake he could see Charley paddling
a canoe in which Helen sat trolling for bass.
He had breakfasted leisurely, and after declin-
ing Burton's invitation to join him and Mrs.

Elting for a sail, settled himself to read the story he and Madge had begun the day before. But it failed to interest him as it had done, and throwing the book aside, he wandered off into the woods and did not come back until late in the afternoon. On his return he found Vinton asleep in his tent and Madge alone in the hammock, reading. She had read to the point where he had put aside the book, and at his request she continued reading aloud. At once his interest awakened, and in the two hours before dinner, he quite forgot how miserable he had been. He watched her as she read, and realized that there had come into his life a passion such as he had never known before. For the time at least he would be happy, forgetting his determination to start with Burton in two days for the mines.

Madge and Ferris walked in silence for some distance after leaving the camp. The trail was broad and well-trodden, and they did not need the lantern, which he carried unlighted. She was the first to speak.

"What are you so busily thinking about?" she asked.

"I was thinking of our former walk over this trail," he answered.

"How well you are getting," she said; "I

will confess now that I was quite alarmed about you then."

"That is too bad. I seem to have come as the one shadow over your bright camp life. But," he added, after a moment's silence, "I am going day after to-morrow, and you will have only the impression of the discomfort I have made you—which I am sure the next three weeks of pleasure will efface."

Fortunately for Madge, it was too dark for Ferris to see the expression of her face as she answered quietly : "I am very sorry. Will you come again before we break camp?"

"I had not intended to do so," he said, adding after a moment's pause, "but if you wish it, I will."

"Indeed, we shall all be delighted to see you, and I am sure the perfect rest here must be of benefit after your busy city life. Or perhaps you have other plans for a vacation?"

"No, I have no plans. I had not thought of getting an outing this fall, but as Captain Vinton was so near, I could not resist the chance to be with him. You know he is both father and friend to me, and has been since I can remember, for my own father died when I was a very small child."

"I envy you such a friendship. I have known him less than two weeks and yet I feel

as if I had known him always. If I were a believer in the transmigration of souls, I should be
sure that in some former state our lives had met.
Do you believe in such things?"

"No; I think we sometimes find such a belief convenient in explaining the suddenness
with which a strong attraction comes into our
lives. A passion on short notice seems shallow,
and we resent it and seek some extraordinary
reason for it. It would be better, I think, if we
simply accepted the fact without attempting to
excuse or explain it. Human passion is as di-
verse as the human face, yet we treat it as if it
were cast for all in the same mould, and that a
a very flat one. Can you not conceive of two
people — strong characters, if you please — dis-
covering their affinity on a week's intimacy as
certainly and truly as the same perception might
come to two others of different temperaments,
in years?"

"Yes, but you must admit that it is less usual
and conventional."

"That is true, yet it need be none the less
strong. To illustrate : Do you think that when
Miss Whitney and Tom Moulton discover — as
they eventually will — that they care very much
for each other, that their affection will be stronger
or more sincere than that of yourself and Captain Vinton?"

"Perhaps not," answered Madge; "though it may not be the same. Will you wait here," she added, as they had now reached the river, "while I examine the river bank for a short distance to see if I can discover any signs of the wanderer? I will return within an hour."

It required but a moment for Madge to light the lantern and hurry away, leaving Ferris on the spot where they had forded the river less than a week before.

Did she love Vinton? This was the question that filled his thoughts. Had she not practically confessed as much in what she had already said? And yet, why should she emphasize the difference between her feeling for Vinton and that of Moulton for Miss Whitney? These and many like questions he vainly sought to answer during the hour or more that he spent in walking restlessly to and fro in the clearing of the river bank at which the logging road ended. But one conclusion he reached. He would discover whether she loved Vinton, even if it necessitated his telling her of his own feelings. He could not go away in the wretchedness of uncertainty.

Having determined on this course, he awaited anxiously her return, for even in the face of what seemed to him certain failure, he could not but cherish a faint hope of success, and this brought a measure of cheerfulness. Lighting a cigar, he began to fancy by degrees that Madge, if she did not love Vinton, might in time learn to care for himself.

From time to time after she had left him, he noticed the signal shots fired at intervals by the searchers beyond the lake, but now the small new-born hope filled his heart and he no longer heard them nor thought of the lost Moulton.

Suddenly there was splashing of water at a little distance above, and Madge's cheerful voice called excitedly:

"Isn't it fortunate they have found him so soon? We must hurry back to camp and get ready the best our larder affords."

"Why do you think they have found him?" asked Ferris, without displaying any great degree of enthusiasm, for the learning of his own fate seemed more important to him than the finding of Moulton, and he knew that a hasty return to camp would prevent his speaking as he had determined.

"Did you not hear the three quick shots? That was to be the signal of success. I was on the other side of the river when I heard them, and I was so impatient to get back that I could not take the time to go up stream to the old log over which I had crossed, and so waded across in the shallowest water I could find. Whew! but it was cold."

"You should not have done that. You ought not to take such chances with your health."

"Never fear for me. We shall be in camp in ten minutes, and between the warmth of the camp fire and Helen's greeting, I shall forget my wet feet. Do you feel strong enough to walk so rapidly?" she asked, slackening the quick pace at which they had started.

"O, yes, I am quite well again," answered Ferris. "At least physically. What makes you so happy to-night?" he asked, as they neared the camp. "Let me share it with you, for I am not very happy."

"Then I will tell you," she answered, "though if you were a woman, you would not need to be told. You would know it; you would feel it in the air. Can't you see how these two people love each other? And do you not experience a touch of reflected happiness? It is beautiful, it is ideal. Is it strange that I share my friend's happiness?"

"No, but are you sure that it is the reflection only that gladdens your heart?"

"It must be; it cannot be anything more for me. Do not take even that away, I beg of you," answered Madge slowly, and as they approached the camp-fire a few moments later, Ferris could see a touch of sadness in her face.

That Helen had heard the signal was evident

as she kissed Madge, who hurried into their tent
for dry shoes and stockings.

"I knew he would be as hungry as a bear,
Madge, and with Dan'l's help I have set out a
delicious supper for him, although he does not
deserve it after causing us all so much anxiety.
Really, it is not safe to trust him alone in the
woods. He won't carry a compass, and if he
did, he would not know how to use it."

"Then you must see to it that he does not
go alone again," answered Madge.   "What a
trial that will be to you," she added with a smile.
"But they have found him, and come very close,
Helen dear, while I whisper something.   You
have found him, too."

"What nonsense you are talking, Madge,"
answered Helen, the color coming to her cheeks.
"Tom,— I mean Mr. Moulton,—and I have
been the best of friends for years."

"Yes, but that is over now, dear. You have
lost your friend and have found —" But Helen
quickly put her hand over Madge's mouth, and
before she could speak again, hurried from the
tent.

Tom Moulton presented a forlorn spectacle
as he wearily climbed the steps that led from the
landing to the camp. He was without hat or
coat ; his shirt and trousers were torn, and his
face and hands badly scratched by the under-

brush through which he had travelled. When found by Whitney and Joe, he was within a few hundred yards of the deserted cabin and was hurrying away from it in his effort to locate the signal shots that Vinton was firing a half mile nearer camp. As they passed the cabin, he insisted on picking up the autumn leaves he had left there. "I shall look less dismal with this patch of color," he said in excuse, and held on to them persistently until he laid them in front of Helen's seat at the dining table.

"If I had confined my attention to gathering these," he said, dropping into his seat at the table a few minutes later, after he had changed his clothing, "I should not have been in this sorry plight. But I attempted to hunt bears, and this is the result."

"How absurd of you," said Helen, "and what would you have done if you had found one?"

"Rather let me tell you what I actually did," answered Moulton, with as much pride in his tone as his fatigued condition would allow. And during the next half hour he entertained the party gathered in the dining tent, with a graphic account of his hunt and subsequent wanderings.

CHAPTER VIII.

IT was late when Ferris appeared at breakfast the morning after the bear hunt. He found Burton and Madge about to start for orchids.

"Uncle and I are off for one of our old tramps this morning, Mr. Ferris. Won't you join us?" she said, seating herself for a moment near him.

"I will decline on one condition," he answered. "It is that you will give me part of this afternoon. I want to go in search of my fishing rod, which disappeared in the river near where you found me, and which I imagine can easily be recovered. It is an old favorite and I should be sorry to lose it now."

"Surely. How stupid of me not to have thought of it before. I will return for luncheon before two and we can go at three. If you have no plan for the morning let me suggest that you walk over to Twin Lakes. The trail is very plain, and the view from the point is well worth seeing."

" I will do so if Miss Whitney will be my
guide," answered Ferris, turning to Helen as
she took her place at the breakfast table.

An hour later Helen and Ferris started just
as Moulton and Whitney came from their tent.

" Won 't you join us, Tom? " said Ferris as
Moulton came toward them.

" No, thank you, Bob, no more tramps for
me. The trail from our tent to the dining tent
is very distinct, and I shall content myself with
following that, for the present at least. I haven't
that confidence in my woodcraft that I had
before yesterday's experience. Besides, I engaged Mrs. Elting last evening for a sail this
morning, and I feel much more confidence on
the water than in the woods."

The Twin Lakes were scarcely more than a
mile from Round Lake, and as the trail ran
through a forest of oak and birch and maple
trees and was free from underbrush, the walk
was an easy one. The point between the two
lakes was a narrow peninsula of high ground,
heavily wooded, from which a view of the
greater part of both lakes could be had. It
was indeed well worth seeing, for the diversity
and richness of coloring along the shores of the
lakes were exceptional even in these woods, which
abounded in such natural beauties. On one
side of the point extended a little bay scarcely

one hundred yards across, covered with lily
pads and fringed with rushes. Beyond this the
lake widened, and from its white sandy beach
the bank rose abruptly and was covered with a
great variety of hard wood, with here and there
a tall pine reaching its branches of dark green
high above the surrounding trees. In places
the white trunks of the silver birch stood out
in bold contrast against a rugged background
of browns and green, and close to the water's
edge a few of the maples were showing the first
touches of the autumn glory. The shores of
the other lake were lower, and near its upper
end the remains of fallen and dead trees showed
where at some former time a beaver dam had
existed, while upon one side a treeless stretch,
densely covered with berry bushes in rank growth,
from which an occasiónal charred stump raised
itself, told of some forest fire that had run to
the water's edge.

As Helen and Ferris walked out onto the
point, a flock of wood duck startled from
the little bay circled in swift flight until they
were high enough to rise over the timber.

"Won't you try a shot at them with my rifle?"
asked Helen, as she saw them swinging overhead. "It is very light, and I am sure you could
manage it with one arm."

"No, thank you," he answered, "I should

surely miss.   Besides I am devoid of aggressive-
ness to-day, even to the extent of not caring
for a shot at ducks.   Let us sit here a while and
see if they do not return.   Can you imagine a
more perfect picture of quietude than this?"

"No.   But indeed these woods are beautiful
and restful beyond any place I have ever known.
I have often wondered at Miss Seaton's enthusiasm for them.   I understand it now.   When
we were in Berlin last winter she sighed for the
woods.   In the galleries she would often stop
before a forest scene by some master artist ;
yet the comment invariably came, 'Yes, this
is beautiful, but not like our woods.'   She is a
very unusual woman, is she not?"

"Yes, I have never known one like her,"
replied Ferris.

"It seems strange to me that she has never
married.   She has so many traits that should
attract men.   Yet while she has many men
friends, I doubt if she ever had an offer of marriage.   I should think that a man would need
to have a goodly measure of conceit to consider himself worthy of her."

Ferris colored slightly as he answered :
"Your doubts are in a fair way to be dispelled,
are they not?"

"I don't think I quite understand," Helen
replied.   "Perhaps I am not very observing.

Would you have me infer that you are bold enough ; you, the woman-hater?"

"Indeed I was not thinking of myself," he said, with embarrassment, his color deepening to a positive blush.

"Surely you cannot mean Captain Vinton? Verily, you are ignorant of a woman's heart, Mr. Ferris. She is fond of him ; so am I ; but can you imagine my loving him? It would be quite as probable."

"No; but for a very different reason," replied Ferris, recovering his self-possession. "It is because you — shall I tell you why?"

"No, Sir Impudence," she answered lightly, now coloring in her turn. "Besides, it would be a very poor return for a piece of information that you should be very glad to get."

"Yes, I should be, if—," and he paused, for the thought that she was learning his inmost secret was not pleasant.

"If you had the courage to admit what you know to be true. What odd creatures you men are. Theoretically, you believe in love, yet when it comes into your lives you meet it with doubt, and fear, and trembling. You try to reason about it and measure it, and altogether deal with it as with the ordinary affairs of life, instead of recognizing it as a power beyond the reach of reason. If it be truly the remnant of original godliness that is left to us, why seek to compass it with the bonds of human reason? We women are wiser in this one thing. We know love's presence intuitively. We do not attempt to explain it, much less doubt it. When a woman doubts if she is in love, you may be sure she is not, or won't be long; whereas with a man it is a sure sign that he is, or soon will be. As I say, we women know such things intuitively ; and sometimes," she added with a roguish smile, " our intuitions are not always with regard to ourselves only."

So far as his feeling for Madge was concerned, Ferris had passed beyond the condition of doubt. He knew that he loved her, but, even with the assurance of Helen to the contrary, he still questioned if she did not love Vinton. This much, at least, he would determine in the afternoon ; yet what Helen had said gave him hope such as he had not known before. He was willing to try to win Madge's love if she was indeed heart free. It was not vanity ; it was only the confidence that a love so great, so enduring as he felt his to be, must find response. But he did not enjoy the personal turn the conversation had taken, and was seeking to change it, when Helen called his attention to an object in the water near the opposite shore of the smaller one of the lakes. He recognized it at once as a deer, although only the head appeared above the water.

"He is swimming this way," he said, after watching it a moment through the field glass, "and will probably cross on the point. If so, you may get a fair shot as he passes us."

But a moment later the deer changed his course and headed for the shore of the lake just beyond the little bay.

"Raise the sights of your rifle," said Ferris; "you can get a snap shot as he leaves the water. It will not be over two hundred yards."

Helen did as she was directed and excitedly waited for the deer to reach the shore.

"Now be ready for him. You must lose no time when he touches land, for it is plain from the way he swims that he has been startled."

As he spoke the deer turned quickly from the shore and headed again towards the point, and for the first time Ferris saw the cause of his alarm. On the edge of the brush, near where the deer was about to leave the water, a timber wolf was skulking, but being to the windward, the deer had got his scent.

"There is his pursuer," said Ferris in an undertone, showing Helen the wolf; "a more dreaded enemy than man, even. Would you rather take a long shot at him?"

"It looks like a great dog — is it a wolf?" asked Helen, now all excitement.

" Yes, and a very large one, I should say."

" Pray, shoot him. I am so excited that it would be folly for me to attempt it ; see how my hand trembles," said Helen ; and it was indeed true, for she could scarcely hold the rifle.

Thrusting his hunting knife into the side of the stump near which they were sitting, in order to give a rest for the gun, Ferris readjusted the sights for three hundred yards — the distance as near as his practiced eye could judge to a little opening in the brush across which he saw the wolf would pass — and as the animal showed himself, he carefully aimed and fired.

"He is gone," said Helen; " I saw him jump. It is too bad."

" But I think I hit him. Do you mind waiting here while I go and see?"

" Might he not come this way?" asked Helen, alarmed at the thought of being left alone.

" There's not the slightest danger of his doing so. If I missed, he is probably a mile away already," answered Ferris. And thus reassured, Helen was content to remain and signal with her handkerchief when Ferris reached the spot where the wolf disappeared. Leaving the rifle with her, he hurried around the edge of the bay.

As he neared the point that he had marked to look for his game, the rifle again rang out and he saw Helen looking in the opposite direction. Standing on the edge of the lake, he called to her, and she answered that she had fired at and missed a beautiful buck. A little further on he came to the open place in which he last saw the wolf, and in the brush beyond he found the animal prostrate and dying, for the bullet had crashed through his spine. Returning to Helen, he found her radiant with excitement.

"Did you get your quarry?" she asked, hurriedly.

"Yes, but are you sure you missed yours?"

"Of course, and it seems so stupid, after I have been practicing in a rifle gallery for a month before coming here, and for this very shot. I was watching you when suddenly I heard a crash in the brush near the water's edge on the other side of the point. To say that I was startled, but mildly expresses my sensation. Of course, I thought it must be the wolf and I was about to call to you when a great buck came dashing towards me. Evidently he was quite as surprised at seeing me as I was at the sight of him, for he stopped an instant within a few rods of me, and then ran through the open timber. As he turned I raised the gun and fired, but he disappeared. It was such an easy

shot.   He had just passed that great pine when
I fired.   We must go back to camp now.   I am
glad we do not return empty handed."

"Walk slowly along the trail we came, and I
will join you in a few minutes," said Ferris, as
he hurried in the direction the deer had taken.
Skilled as he was in hunting big game, he found
no difficulty in following the fresh tracks of the
buck in the soft earth and pine needles, but he
was about to conclude that Helen had, indeed,
missed when he came upon a pool of fresh
blood along the trail.   It was plain that the
animal was wounded, and from the fact that he
did not bleed at once, he knew that the hemor-
rhage was internal and the wound a bad one.
Noting the spot, he joined Helen and they were
soon in camp.

At the landing Joe was busily engaged in
whittling out a paddle of white birch, but with
a few hurried directions from Ferris, he dropped
his work, took his pack straps and, calling to
Charley in Chippewa, the two disappeared in
the direction of Twin Lakes.

As the party finished luncheon an hour later,
Joe called Ferris aside and told him that he and
Charley had brought in both the wolf and the
buck and .hung them on the beach beyond the
landing.   At the table Helen had given a graphic
account of their morning's adventure, sounding

the praises of Ferris's marksmanship and lament-
ing her own lack of skill.   Ferris now invited
all to view the game, but allowed Helen and
Moulton to go first, that the surprise might be
the more complete.

*   *   *   *   *   *

Leaving their fellow-campers to their own
devices after luncheon, Ferris and Madge went
to the river in search of the lost rod.   Madge
had brought with her a trolling line with a
heavy spoon-hook, and after a few unsuccessful
casts across the pool at the edge of which
Ferris had met with his accident, the spoon
caught in his line, which had been carried
down stream, doubtless by a trout, as the
sombre "brown- hackle" was the only fly left
upon the leader.   The rod was found unbroken,
and after stretching the line to dry, they
wandered up stream until they reached the
fallen tree, which made an easy bridge between
the banks.

"I will show you one of my favorite old
haunts," said Madge, as they crossed the stream.
"It is only a little way from the river.   When
Uncle Tom and I camped here I used to spend
many hours there while he was hunting and
botanizing. It was beautiful then, and I imagine
must be so still.   Time makes very little change
in these dear old woods.   Uncle Tom called

this my throne," she said, a moment later, as they reached the brow of the little hill, on the very top of which three tall Norway pines grew a few feet apart, forming a small triangular space, in which Burton years before had built a rustic bench.

Brushing away the leaves and pine needles that had accumulated upon it, Madge seated herself.

"Won't you share my throne with me?" she said lightly. "It is really not so rough and uncomfortable as it looks."

Ferris stood before her a moment in admiration. With such environment she was indeed beautiful. His heart was beating so fast that he could scarcely speak, and yet his whole soul was seeking utterance. She looked into his eyes and the color crept into her cheeks. If possible, she would have stopped the flood of passion that was sweeping toward her. But it was too late. He came quite close and, looking earnestly at her as she sat with her eyes downcast and her hands clasped in her lap, said very gently and slowly, his voice tremulous as he spoke:

"My queen, I want to share your life with you. You told me last night that love made its presence known. If that is true, you must know, in a measure, what I feel, better than any words can tell. My heart has been saying three little words so fast, so constantly, that they seem to have crowded out all other words as they have all other thought — I love you; I love you."

"No, no, do not say that, I beg. You must not. Indeed you must not. It can mean but wretchedness for you — for both of us. I know, Mr. Ferris, the truth of what I say. Forget that you have spoken to me of this, and let us go back to camp."

As she spoke, she rose. Her eyes met his, and he saw her utter unhappiness.

"It is too late," he said sadly. " I know that I love you. It is the one certainty of my life. I feared that it might be hopeless — that you cared for another. Yet I could not help telling you. Fool that I was, to think that a miserable fellow like myself, who has never had the art to win a woman's smile, should aspire to your love. But you have filled my life since I have known you. I would work so hard for you; I would wait so patiently for you; I would try to be as other men whom women care for — if only sometime, perhaps, ever so long from now, I could hope to win you. Tell me that you love another, and I will go away; or if you do not, let me hope, let me try. Do not send me away."

As he spoke, Madge sank hopelessly to the seat and covered her eyes with her hands. She was silent for a moment, but Ferris could see that he had caused her to weep, and an infinite sadness came over him.

"I am sorry, dear, that I have made you so unhappy. Tell me that there is another, and I will leave you. You will forget that I have made this shadow in your holiday, and I — I — my God, I will live on — "

"No, no, Robert, do not speak like that; I cannot bear it. Indeed, I cannot," she cried, looking him full in the face and brushing the tears from her eyes. "There is no other — there has never been another — I love you. I seem to have loved you always. No, no, do not take my hand. Listen to me, Robert, for I must tell you why you shall not love me, though it breaks my heart."

"Say what you will, now, darling. Your voice will be music even if you speak my doom."

He sat on the bed of soft pine needles at her feet, and leaning against the seat, rested his hand on a fold of her dress, — for it was part of her. He could have been happy now, come what might, except for the sorrow that overwhelmed her, for she had said she loved him, and this was all his heart could compass.

"Oh! Robert, if I might only forget for a little while; if I might hear you say you love me, and forget that I can never claim your love, — I

would willingly bear a lifetime of wretchedness.
But you must go away from me, Robert,
dear—"

"Never, my darling."

"Yes, but you must, and you must forget me.
Oh! that is the hardest thought of all. It is
dreadful, but I must have courage to tell you.
Please do not look at me so,—do not look up
again until I have finished, and then you must
bid me good-bye. Robert, you have heard me
call Dr. Burton my uncle. He is not; I am
nobody's child. I am—"

"You are mine, dearest. Do not think of
the past again. Forget it. Let us think only
of the future that holds so much in store for us
now. There can be no one to claim your love
but me, and in return I will give you in such
measure that you shall not miss the love of
others."

"Do not tempt me, Robert, to forget a vow
that is part of my conscience. I made it years
ago, when I was a mere child and scarcely old
enough to appreciate the wretchedness it might
bring. No, no, I shall never accept the love of
any man, unless I know that my blood is free
from the taint of sin. If I loved you less it
would be easier to break this vow, to think only
of my own happiness, to flatter myself that I
could make you forget that the woman you loved

was a waif,— a child of the street, maybe. Gladly would I risk all, the chiding of my own conscience, the waning of your love, if my happiness alone were at stake, but I will not jeopardize yours. It may seem hard to you now, dearest, but some day,— a long, long time from now, you will realize that I am right. You must go away now. You must forget to-day. Forget that you have told me of your love. In time you will find some one more worthy to receive this great gift, and I will pray for that time, Robert, with my whole heart. I did not mean that you should know that I love you. It would have been easier for you had I not done so. But leave me now, and I will bid you good-bye to-morrow."

While Madge spoke thus, slowly and with tears in her voice, the old look of determination came back to Ferris's face, and with earnestness he said:

"Do you think, dear, that I can lose you now? You do not know my heart; I cannot believe that what you dread is true. Tell me what you know of your life, and I will prove,— if it takes the best years of my life,— that your fears are groundless. Only let me know all, and I will begin to-morrow."

For an instant a look of happiness, born of hope, came into her face, but it passed as quickly.

"There is little to tell. When I was but a

few months old, my mother was shipwrecked on the Delaware coast. It was in September of 1862. The vessel, 'La Stella,' sailed from Lisbon in July. My mother and I were the only passengers, and of the crew, all were lost except two sailors. Dr. Burton took my mother and me to his home, and soon after that she died. Of my father I have never been able to learn anything — not even his name. Before she died she asked that I might be called Margery Seaton — the same name that marks her grave. Years ago, when I learned that Dr. Burton was not related to me, I sought to learn more of my father, but he discouraged the attempt, for he could give me no hope of success. Last fall I went to Lisbon. I searched for weeks for some clue, but in vain. I found the name of Seaton only once in the church register and that was many years before I was born. A woman of that name had married the British Consul, who died a few years afterwards, and of his descendants I could learn nothing. I paid men to help me in my search. We found the record of the vessel, but it did not show that on her last voyage she carried any passengers. No, I cannot see a ray of hope."

"Do not despair, dearest. Let me take up the search. I feel that I shall succeed. May I talk with Dr. Burton before I begin? You know this means everything to me.   And when I succeed, as I know I shall — "

" Then come back to me, Robert, and I will give you such love as never woman gave before. Yes, you may tell Uncle Tom, but not Captain Vinton.   It would grieve him, and he is devoted to you beyond all else in the world."

Many were the questions that Ferris put to Madge in the hope of getting some further clue to her parentage.   While he discovered little that could be of service to him in his search, his inquiries awakened in Madge a new hope, for they served to show her how much more clever and systematic would be his method of conducting the search than hers had been.

The shadows were deepening in the woods, the sunlight touching only the tops of the taller pines, when they realized that it was time to return to camp.   After crossing the river Ferris picked up his rod, and as they walked along Madge slowly wound in the line upon his reel. When this was done, he said :   "You will keep these, Madge dear, until I come again ?"

For an hour they had almost forgotten that there could be any doubt as to his return. These words brought again to Madge the thought that he might never come back to her and she answered sadly :   "Yes, Robert. But if you should not return ?"

"Do not question, dearest; I know that I shall. My only dread is that the time may be long, but I shall not fail."

As they neared the camp they walked more slowly, reluctant that this last sweet meeting should end. Almost in sight of camp they stopped.

"Robert, dear," Madge held out her hand to him and he saw tears in her eyes as he took it.

"Not 'good-bye,' darling, but 'courage';" he drew her gently to him and the first kiss of love of these two strong hearts was given.

A moment later they reached the camp and found the dinner awaiting them. All but Whitney were in camp. He had gone duck-shooting and would no doubt be absent so long as there was daylight enough for him to see the sights of his gun. Helen and Moulton were watching the Indians pile up the logs for the evening camp-fire, the size of which grew with the increasing coldness of the autumn nights. Mrs. Elting was busy writing a letter, and Burton and Vinton were sitting on an old log near the cook's tent chatting away like old-time friends, for camp life is a rapid developer of affinities.

A few vigorous raps by old Dan'l on the bottom of a tin pan announced dinner and brought the party together at the table. For the first time since he joined the party, Ferris was in high spirits and, as Vinton said, "quite like his old self." His going in the morning was not mentioned during the meal. Helen knew that he and Madge had spent the afternoon together, and with quick intuition divined the cause of his happiness ; and once or twice when Ferris caught her eyes he felt the color come into his cheeks and his heart beat faster. Yet he knew that in her his secret had a safe custodian.

The camp fire was snapping briskly in the crisp air as they gathered around it after dinner, the sparks chasing each other into the leafy darkness above until lost in the high boughs of the old hemlock that stretched over and beyond the smaller trees. As they left the table, Whitney appeared with a good bag of ducks, which he hung with reluctance on the game rack ; he would have preferred to spread them out for the admiration of the others, since he alone had contributed to the replenishment of the larder. But appetite was stronger than pride, and after a hurried toilet he joined the Indians and Dan'l at their meal.

The chill night air, which promised a heavy frost, brought all close about the fire. Ferris found a place on the rug beside Madge, where, by turning his back to the fire he could watch her face ; to-night it was radiant. Helen and Moulton occupied a rustic settee mounted on rude

rockers, but withal very comfortable and dedicated to the "orchestra," as Moulton dubbed
Helen and himself. It was an ideal night; not
a cloud was in the sky, and the myriads of stars
showed through the leaves and open places and
found reflection on the surface of the lake, which
was rippled by the faintest breeze.

Moulton tuned his banjo and found vent for
his excess of spirits in a number of topical songs
that he had been lucky enough to get hold of
before they became too familiar. Then Helen
and he sang together, and later he improvised an
accompaniment to the "Canadian Boat Song,"
and others of those good old-fashioned choruses
which all knew and the simple harmonies of
which invited all to join. Vinton, too, in a
crude but melodious baritone, sang a rhythmical
old Spanish boat song that drew Dan'l from his
dishes.

Vinton noticed him in the shadow across the
camp-fire as he finished, and said: "It's a long
time, Dan'l, since you heard that song."

"Ay, sor, nigh twenty-seven years; but it's
mighty good to hear your voice again."

Dan'l returned to his dishes; but the memory
awakened by the old song absorbed Vinton's
thought, and soon after he drew his top coat over
his shoulders and strolled down to the landing.
A little later Madge said a general good-night

to all, and as she leaned over in rising from the
rug, whispered a special "good-night, Robert
dear," very softly; so softly, indeed, that only
one heard it, but his heart beat fast with happiness for an hour afterwards.

Helen and Mrs. Elting went with Madge, and
Whitney and Moulton disappeared in their tent
arm in arm, humming the chorus of an old college song.   Ferris remained by the fire a short
time and then sought Vinton to tell him of his
departure.   It was a sad disappointment to his
old friend, for they had had no fishing or hunting together; but no argument or thought of
pleasure could change Ferris' plans.   As they
were parting for the night Vinton said :

"There is another reason, Robert, why I am
sorry to have you go. You are nearer to me, boy,
than any one else ; you are as my own child.   I
had hoped that perhaps you might care for Miss
Seaton ; she is such a noble girl."

Gladly would he have told Vinton all, but for
the promise to Madge.   As it was, he simply
answered :

"Do not worry about me, Uncle Phil. Sometime I may surprise you, for indeed, I am not
as indifferent to women as I am credited with
being."

CHAPTER IX.

IT is always an unpleasant incident of camp life to have one of the party leave; it is like losing a member of one's family, and the return to civilization seems quite like going to a far-away country. When Ferris announced his departure at the breakfast table the next morning it was received with a storm of protest. But for him there was now only one object — the winning of Madge — and he was impatient to talk with Burton and begin the search upon the success of which his happiness depended. It was a disappointment to him, therefore, when he found that Burton had arranged to have Joe take him back to the cabins by the river route, which would consume the entire day. He protested that he was strong enough to make the journey through the woods, but Burton insisted that he should go by the river, and as Madge favored this plan, he reluctantly yielded.

Whitney had started at daylight with Charley to investigate a lake some ten miles away that gave promise of good shooting. The others, with the exception of Mrs. Elting, walked with Ferris to the river and part way to the rapids, where he was to take the canoe. He had stated as the reason for his departure, that there was an important matter requiring his attention, and all except Madge thought it had to do with the labor troubles, and asked no questions.

"I do hope, Robert," said Vinton, as they were about to part, "that, if possible, you will join us again. Now promise me that if you can finish your work before we break camp you will come back."

"Indeed I will. If I succeed before you are out of the woods I shall take the first train for Keating. The errand is urgent and may require some time for its accomplishment — but I am confident," he added, looking at Madge, "that in the end I shall succeed."

"No doubt of that, my boy, for you always do ; but see that the end is reached soon, so that we may have you again. Will you stop long at Keating, or go at once to Chicago ?"

"To Chicago direct, and after a day there I shall probably go East for a few days, at least. I shall see you in Chicago if I fail to meet you here again."

As Madge gave him her hand, she said simply : "I trust we shall meet again very soon."

A furtive glance at her face as she spoke told Helen that the girl's heart had gone with Ferris.

For some time after they left the party, Ferris and Joe walked on in silence, the Indian in advance. Suddenly the latter stopped and looking back said eagerly: "Man come." A moment later Vinton was seen hurrying toward them.

"I will walk a little way with you," he said. "It occurred to me, after you said you would go East, that probably you would be in New York. If so, I want you to do something for me. This is the key to my box in the Surety Company's office. You know Judge Durham, the president; he will see that you get access to it. In the front of the box you will find a small leather case. If you come here before we break camp bring it with you; otherwise, keep it in Chicago until I see you. Be careful of it, Robert, for it is of great value to me by reason of its associations."

Vinton accompanied Ferris and Joe to the rapids and watched them disappear beyond the bend of the river. Then turning toward camp, he said musingly: "How like his father. I seem almost to be living my youth over again."

Burton did not start for his cabin until after luncheon. Madge walked with him several miles but she was depressed and talked little.

"What is it that troubles you, Madge?" he asked, as she was about to leave him. "Isn't the camp congenial?"

"Oh, yes. The trouble is with myself. I am a coward; I did not know that I was so weak. I am weighed down by a feeling of loneliness such as I have never known. It is foolish, I know, uncle dear, and you have been so good to me. But I cannot help it to-day. To-morrow, perhaps, I shall be stronger."

"You must not feel so, child. I will go back to camp with you and send Charley to meet Ferris and explain my absence. There is no real necessity for my going."

"Yes, but there is, I am sure. He would not go without seeing you. Indeed, I know he would not."

Burton turned as she spoke. He saw the color mount to her temples and, taking her hands, said:

"What does this mean, Madge dear? Look at me, child. Do you love him?"

Her eyes filled with tears, but she smiled sadly through them, as she answered slowly:

"All ·the love that I have not given you, uncle, is his. Do not ask me more. He will tell you all, and you will know why I am so wretched. Good-bye, uncle dear. Come day after to-morrow, if you can, and you will find

me your own old Madge again." And brushing
the tears from her eyes, she turned and walked
slowly back over the trail.

Burton stood for a moment undecided
whether to return with her or go on, then
reluctantly resumed his journey. As he pon-
dered over what Madge had said, he became
more and more perplexed. It did not occur
to him at first that Ferris might not love her,
but as he considered how utterly miserable she
seemed, the possibility of some such untoward
complication suggested itself. Else why was
she so unhappy, and why was he so anxious to
leave the camp? Burton had conceived a strong
attachment for Ferris in the short time he had
known him, and could not believe that he was
the man to seek to win a woman's love unless
his own were given in return. Madge he knew
to be in earnest, and he knew, too, that whatever the obstacle in the way of her union with
Ferris, it was to her a real and, as she believed,
an insurmountable one. His one great concern
was for her happiness. The fact that the realiza-
tion of that happiness would take her from him,
did not lessen his desire that it should be at-
tained. Since the death of his wife she had
been the centre of his thoughts; had she been
his own child, he could not have lavished upon
her a greater devotion. What could it be that

stood between her and her love for Ferris? Again and again he found himself asking this question, as he hastened toward his cabins.

It was nearly six o'clock when he reached them and found that Ferris and Joe had arrived an hour before. Ferris had changed his clothing and was watching Adam prepare the dinner. The old negro was not inclined to be talkative, but when Ferris told him how Madge had found him with his arm broken and had taken him into camp, and how kind she had been to him since, his eyes brightened and his face showed the affection with which he regarded her.

"She never told me that, sah, when she come here after Mister Thomas. She jes' said you had broke your arm, but she didn't give herself no credit. But it's jes' like her. She allus was a cur'ous child ever since she was a little baby."

"Have you known her so long as that, Adam?" Ferris asked.

"Yes, indeed, sah. I knowed her when she fust come. I mean when Mister Thomas saved her and her ma from the wreck of the 'Stella.' Lord, sah, that was a tur'ble day. You oughter git Mister Thomas to tell you 'bout it. I was brought up on the marsh, but I never see sech a storm as we had that time. Out of the whole crew of the vessel there was only two saved besides Miss Madge and her ma, and they'd a gone, too, if Mister Thomas hadn't saved 'em. That seems a long time ago, Mister Ferris, and I'm getting to be a purty ole man, but I can't never forget that day as long as I live."

"Do you remember her mother?" Ferris next asked.

"Yes, sah, she lived more'n a month after that, but I reckon she never got over the cold she ketched at that time. She was 'xactly like Miss Madge in her looks, 'ceptin' a good deal paler, but I don't b'lieve you could a tole 'em apart. When I seen Miss Madge come over here the other night paler'n a sheet and a laying in her bed like she was dead, I tell you, sah, it give me the creeps, she looked so much like her ma when she was laid out. Poor child, but she never missed her ma, for Mister Thomas he's been same as one to her all'us."

There were tears in the old negro's eyes, and he might have broken down completely, had not his quick sense of smell detected something burning. He turned just in time to save the fish on the stove, and Ferris, walking to the door, saw Burton coming from the woods across the bridge.

If Burton had entertained any question as to Ferris's honesty of heart, it disappeared when he looked into his clear gray eyes and felt the earnest grasp of his hand. Ferris noticed that he was looking unusually serious, but attributed it to the fatigue of his long tramp.

"It will probably be a half hour before dinner, and I must take a look at your arm. Perhaps I can relieve you of the splints," said Burton, as they went into his room.

"Indeed, I hope so," Ferris replied, "for I shall have need of both hands and of my head, too, in the work that is before me."

Burton looked him squarely in the face, and seeing the earnest questioning expression, Ferris added with a half-smile, the color coming to his cheeks as he spoke:

"I will tell you what this work is, Doctor, for it concerns you as well as myself. You have helped me before, and I am sure you can in this. It has to do with Miss Seaton and her happiness as well as mine. I have asked her to be my wife."

Ferris paused, and a smile of relief came into Burton's face, but it passed as Ferris added: "She has refused to marry me until she knows more about her parentage. My work now is to learn of it. Perhaps I should have consulted you before I spoke to her, but, to be frank with you, I was in no mood to act deliberately, though your opinion of me might then have been more favorable."

"No, it would not have been. I am conceited enough to value my own estimate of a man, and I have liked you, Robert, since we first met. I will help you so far as I possibly can, and most gladly."

But Burton, even as he spoke, realized the nature of the condition that stood between Ferris and his happiness. He knew that Madge would not alter her determination, and he believed that the attempt to establish her legitimacy must end in failure or worse. In his professional work he had learned that oftentimes the most beautiful and attractive children are born outside the bonds of marriage; so that Madge's charms of mind and body brought no argument to him as they did to Ferris.

"From what you know, do you think we shall be successful?" Ferris asked.

Burton paused a moment, for he could not find it in his heart to say what he really thought. He answered:

"Let me think about it until after dinner. We will talk it over then."

Burton found that Ferris's arm had healed so rapidly that he could safely remove the splints, which he did upon condition that for at least a week he would wear it in a sling. There was but little conversation at dinner, for each was absorbed in his own schemes for solving the problem that was now all-important to both.

In Burton's room they sipped their coffee in silence in front of the small fire on the open hearth. It seemed a long time to Ferris since last he had sat in that room, although in fact only a week had passed. But in that short time the purpose of his life had changed. Then the most absorbing motive was his work and the study incident to it; now these seemed trivial compared with the task that lay between him and the gaining of Madge. Burton had lighted a cigar with Ferris, but after smoking it a few moments he tossed it into the fire, and rising restlessly, filled his pipe.

"I can't think with a cigar. It is too distracting to one who is out of the habit of smoking them, as I am when in the woods," he said, as he resumed his seat.

Ferris rose to set his coffee cup upon the table, and after walking back and forth across the room, drew his chair near Burton's and said:

"What effort have you made to find him?"

"To be honest with you, Robert—but little— and for the reason that it seemed hopeless with the facts I had before me. Had I foreseen what has now happened I might have done differently; but I have always been able to give her everything she needed or wished, and until now I have never realized that the question of her parentage might be of such serious moment to her."

"Why is it that you regard the attempt to find her father as hopeless? Are there no clues whatever?"

"Yes, but I am sorry to say they do not point to success. I will tell you what I know and you can then judge for yourself."

Burton rose from his chair, and, laying his pipe upon the mantel, stood with his back to the fire and his hand over his eyes, as if trying to recall the scenes he was about to recount. After a moment's silence, he said:

"On September 13, 1862, the Spanish brig 'La Stella' was wrecked on the Delaware coast near the town of Lewes. We had been having a succession of storms from the first of the month, which culminated in the gale of the 13th. The Delaware breakwater was at that time incomplete, but it gave fair shelter and was laid down on the charts. For several days much wreckage had come ashore, and the men of the town were well-nigh exhausted with the labor of patrolling the beach. I had been on duty the night of the 12th and was on my way home, when I saw, in the dim light of the dawn, a hull out at sea and in distress. Her mainmast and mizzenmast had completely gone; her foretopmast, also, had been blown away, and a ragged jib was the only sail she carried. As it grew lighter we could see that she was making for the breakwater, but her hull was well down and her progress slow. By nine o'clock she had come so near that with a strong glass we could see the men at the pumps and we believed that she would make the anchorage all right. When within two miles of the breakwater, the captain, who was at the wheel, was washed overboard, and the man who took his place was evidently ignorant of the coast, for he altered her course and headed her directly for the point of shoals inside the cape. We tried by signals to have them stand farther out, but our signals were either not seen or were misunderstood, for in half an hour the brig was hard aground with every sea washing over her decks. There were but eight men left of the crew and of these only two reached shore alive. The ship's boats had evidently been carried away in the gale, and the men jumped into the sea with such wreckage as they could find. It was impossible, as the sea was running, to launch a boat in the surf, and we could offer no help whatever.

" After the ship was deserted, as we thought, I saw a woman come from the forward companionway and climb to the cross-trees of the foremast. How she managed to reach that position without being swept off by the sea was a mystery, but she did, and when there she wedged herself fast in the rigging. Again and again during the forenoon we tried without success to launch a boat. In the afternoon the wind went down somewhat. I could find only four men able to handle a boat. After much difficulty we succeeded in getting through the surf and headed for the wreck, but in our exhausted condition our progress was very slow. We were within hailing distance and were pulling round, for we had drifted to leeward, when one of the oars crabbed and the boat, caught in the trough of the sea, was capsized. My men clung to the boat, but when I came to the surface I found myself at some distance from it, still holding to my oar. I swam for the wreck and at last reached it exhausted, I assure you. Fortunately, the sea, sweeping over the deck, left me there, and I managed to get into the rigging. Then I discovered that the woman had a child bound close to her breast by a woolen scarf or shawl. The child was Madge and she was sleeping as sweetly as if the rocking mast were a cradle. Her mother was almost exhausted from exposure and hunger. I signalled to the men on the shore for help, and more than once I saw them fail in the attempt to launch a boat through the surf. The child awoke and began to cry with hunger, but the exhausted mother could give her no food. My God! I shall never forget that mother's face as her great brown eyes looked despairingly into mine. I tried to encourage her but she had lost hope. For a long time she leaned against me with her eyes closed and her weak hands trying to comfort the sobbing child. At last she cried faintly: 'I am growing cold. Can you keep baby warm?' I tucked the little thing in the front of my woolen shirt and the heat of my body soon soothed her to sleep. The mother smiled faintly and said: 'If you should be saved will you be very good to her? She is so dear to me. How can I leave my child alone? Oh, God, protect her.' I thought she was dying, for her pulse was scarcely perceptible. The darkness was beginning to come on, so that I could hardly see the men on the shore, and although the sea was subsiding somewhat, I had about abandoned hope, when I heard the deep blast of a steamer's whistle, and turning I saw an ocean liner heading for the breakwater and not over half a mile away. I signalled frantically, and you can imagine my sensation when I saw that they had succeeded in lowering a boat and had sent it to our rescue. Just how they managed to get us down from the rigging with the sea running as it was, is still a mystery to me, and I have no recollection of boarding the steamer, which we did behind the breakwater.

When I recovered consciousness I found myself in bed with the child beside me and fast asleep. The ship's surgeon assured me that my child was all right and that my wife (for such he supposed the babe's mother to be) was resting quietly.

" In the morning we went ashore, and I took Madge and her mother to my home. Under the tender care of my wife, Madge grew strong and well, but her mother never recovered from the shock, and although she lived nearly two months, was never able to leave the house. During the first month of her illness, which was typhoid-pneumonia, I did not allow her to talk of matters that might excite her. When her convalescence began she asked permission to write a letter, and when it was finished and sealed, she requested me to direct it to the Secretary of the Navy, which I did. She then told me that she had written to learn the whereabouts of her husband, from whom she had had no word for a long time. She told me also that she had married secretly an American officer against the will of her father, who had died shortly after, leaving her absolutely alone in the world. I might have learned more from her then, but I found that it was taxing her strength to talk of the matter.

" Nearly two weeks passed before any word

came from Washington. During that time she continued slowly to improve and was finally able to sit up. Each day she inquired anxiously for the mail, and I remember the eagerness with which she opened the official envelope that contained the answer to her letter. She had been sitting before the fire with Madge upon her knee as happy as a cricket. As I entered the room, she arose, holding the child in her arms. She read the letter through, and seemed stunned. Again she read it, and then let it fall into the open fire and sank into a chair. I hastened to her, thinking she had fainted, but she had not. She said almost inaudibly, ' Dead, dead; oh, my child, my child.' She lived but two days after that. Before she died she asked me to keep her fatherless child and to call her Margery Seaton. I promised to care for her as my own, and I have tried, Robert, to keep my promise."

Burton paused a moment and, passing his hand across his eyes, continued :

"My wife was an invalid and we had no children of our own, having lost our little girl six months before. For two years I struggled at my profession in Lewes. Then my wife died, and almost immediately thereafter my uncle was killed in the war, leaving to me considerable property in Detroit, to which place I at once removed. I searched the naval register, but found there no officer of the name of Seaton. Several years afterwards I went to Washington and endeavored to find the letter of inquiry, thinking to obtain the real name of Madge's father from that. The letter was not in the files of the department, or at any rate, could not be found. I have made no further effort to ascertain her parentage. I have given you, I think, all the facts in my possession, and I trust that you may see some ray of hope, for I confess I do not. Perhaps in Lisbon, from which port the 'Stella' sailed, something may be learned, but I doubt it."

Ferris was silent for a few moments after Burton had finished. Then he said:

"No, I will begin my search in this country. I will go first to Washington and endeavor to obtain possession of the letter written by Mrs. Seaton to the Secretary of the Navy. Failing to find that, I will learn what ships were stationed at Lisbon or thereabouts at the beginning of our war, and ascertain the names of their officers and of those that were killed or died before that letter was answered. I wish Uncle Phil were going with me; he could help me in this. However, some of my father's friends are stationed in Washington, and I am sure they will serve me. What became of the two sailors who escaped from the wreck?"

"One went to sea again almost immediately. The other is living in New York, or was two years ago, when I ran across him by chance on the street. His name is Vironi and he keeps a sailor's boarding house."

"If I am unsuccessful in Washington, I shall look him up. Perhaps something may be learned from him. Did the mother leave anything that might serve in the way of identification?"

"No, I think not. She had no jewelry, except a small locket containing a knot of brown hair, which she wore on a chain about her neck, and Madge, I think, wears it now. On her left hand she wore a plain gold ring, which was buried with her. I understood from her that everything she possessed was lost in the wreck."

"Was no attempt made to recover the cargo?"

"Not at the time; and within a few days the hull went to pieces, and whatever of the cargo drifted ashore was gathered up by wreckers."

Thus question after question was put to Burton by Ferris, but in the end no new facts were discovered. At last the young man asked:

"From what you saw of Mrs. Seaton, do you believe that she was an honest woman?"

"I am certain of that," was the prompt reply.

"Then why do you doubt that she was married to Madge's father?"

"The fact that she was honest, while tending

to prove that she was married, is by no means conclusive. Every good and pure woman in her inmost soul recognizes love as the supreme prerequisite to marriage. To such, love sometimes comes with so bewildering an intensity that for the time at least the existence of other prerequisites may be forgotten. Under such conditions, when a woman yields the citadel of her heart the surrender may be absolute, if the captor be a dastard. A woman's greatest strength is in her power to love, and therein, too, lies her greatest weakness. I do not say that this was the case with Madge's mother; but the fact that her father for a year gave no sign of his purpose to return and that he apparently deceived her as to his real name, makes me think that in other ways he was false to her. Perhaps the formality of a marriage may have been gone through, but I could never see what was to be gained by establishing it. The man was a villain either in his betrayal of her without marriage or by his desertion of her afterwards. For this reason I have discouraged Madge in her efforts to find him."

It was late when Ferris and Burton parted for the night and much later before Ferris fell asleep. As they were starting for Keating on the following morning, Burton called Ferris to his room and gave him the photograph of Madge.

"Keep this, Robert," he said. "Some day I trust you may claim the original, though she is dearer to me than all else in the world."

At the mine they found John Brent in high spirits. He was as delighted with the new machinery as a child with a new toy, and the results of the first week's work under the tonnage scale gave assurance of the complete fulfillment of their promises to the men. In his inquiries, Ferris did not forget Jack Turnley, who had fully recovered. Brent liked the fellow and was only too glad to carry out Ferris's wishes as to his reinstatement. Their reward was prompt, for when Jack reported for duty after dinner, he thanked them both and then inquired of Brent rather sheepishly if he thought "Mr. Ferris and Doc Burton would be offended if he asked them to the weddin' to-morrow night."

"Thus love will find a way," said Ferris to Burton, with a smile.

"And so may it ever," replied Burton, significantly.

Burton waited to see Ferris aboard the southbound express before leaving the town. It was understood that the latter should report the result of his eastern trip, and as soon as the camping party came out of the woods, Burton would arrange his affairs and join in the search.

"Don't be discouraged, Robert," he said, as

they heard the distant whistle of the train. "There may be a chance of success, and we will not abandon hope until we have exhausted every possible resource."

"Discouraged? Believe me, I am not. It will take years of failure to teach me that word."

As the train drew away from the station, Burton mounted his horse and started for his cabin, pausing a moment on the track to watch the red signal lights on the rear car shining like two great eyes down the long vista of towering pines. Then moving on, he said with a half sigh: "Surely, such courage deserves to win. Hope and youth, how they go hand in hand. When hope dies, youth may not long survive."

CHAPTER X.

A DAY in Chicago was sufficient for Ferris to get his affairs in shape for his Eastern trip, and within twenty-four hours after leaving Keating, he was on the train for Washington. He had taken but ten days' vacation in two years, and his request for two months' leave was readily approved by the president of the company, who congratulated him most heartily on the successful termination of the troubles at the mines.

"Which way are you going, Robert?" he asked, when Ferris had told him that he would start at once.

"To Washington first, and then probably to New York. After that my movements are uncertain."

"There are no elk or bear in either of those places. But perhaps you are in pursuit of fairer game this time," he added, quizzingly.

Ferris colored as he answered evasively: "No, the elk and bear are safe from me this fall."

He had not been in Washington for several years, but when he was a boy Vinton had been stationed there for three years, and his memories of the place were most pleasant. It was dusk as his train neared the city. From the car window he could see the dome of the capitol looming high above the intervening hills and trees and squalid houses between it and the river. There is a personality almost about that towering mass of painted iron that impresses anyone familiar with it. To Ferris it brought back his childhood days when he had romped through its vast vault and climbed its seemingly interminable winding stairway, with Vinton watching him as anxiously as if he were his own.

" Dear old Uncle Phil," he said to himself. " If you were only with me now — when I need you as never before."

At that time — and perhaps it is so now — " The Ebbitt House " was the favored hostelry of the army and navy. As the old manager had known Vinton, Ferris was always sure of a cordial welcome and a comfortable room ; and in these he was not disappointed this time, for the manager greeted him warmly and personally, showed him to " Captain Vinton's old quarters," as he called a suite of rooms high up on the south side and overlooking the monument grounds and the river beyond.

Ferris had dressed for dinner and was standing in front of the open window looking down on the lights of the quiet city, when there was a knock at the door, and a negro servant brought him a card on which was engraved the name " Mr. Francis Herndon," and beneath it the letters " U. S. N."

"Ah !" exclaimed Ferris, with pleasure. " Captain Herndon.   Say that I will be down in a moment."

" Yes, sah, I will ax de *Commodore* to wait in de 'ception room," replied the negro, with emphasis on the officer's title, as he disappeared — a reminder to Ferris that his old friend had at last received the long coveted promotion.

Ferris had known Herndon ever since he could remember, for the latter was one of those fortunate officers who, in some mysterious way, manage to get the choicest assignments, and with the exception of the necessary minimum amount of sea duty, he had been stationed either at Washington or New York during the greater part of his service. He had been a classmate and close friend of Ferris's father and an intimate of Vinton. Ferris had not seen him for several years, but his appearance had changed very little.   He was a stout man, with a floridity of complexion acquired originally by exposure and perpetuated by a generous indulgence in good living — a type not infrequent in army and navy circles. His heart was as young as ever, and his laugh reminded Ferris of the times when he used to see him and Vinton reminiscent over their bottle of ancient Madeira. He greeted Ferris warmly, explaining that he had chanced to see his name on the hotel register on his way to dinner and thought that, as he was alone, they might dine together. His family, he added, were at Newport for the summer. He proved to be the man of all others who could be of assistance to Ferris in his Washington search; for he was on duty at the Navy Department and had easy access to such of its records as might be of service. Without going into details or giving names, Ferris explained to him in a general way that the purpose of his visit was to obtain as full and accurate information as possible regarding the officers of the Mediterranean squadron stationed in proximity to Lisbon in the summer of 1861.

"Our squadron was small at that time, for Congress was as niggardly then as now in the matter of naval appropriations," said Herndon, closing his eyes a moment, as if the revival of such ancient memories was an effort. "There were but four ships in all, and of these I think only the old 'Macedonian' stopped for any considerable length of time at Lisbon. Indeed, I do not now recall that during our stay there any of the others touched even, until we got our sailing orders and waited for the 'Saratoga' to join us. I was junior lieutenant on the 'Macedonian' at that time with Vinton and your father. Lord, Bob, how you resemble him! I loved him as my own brother. But so did all of us, for that matter;" and there was a tone of pathos in the old fellow's voice as he paused.

Then he gave Ferris a list of the officers and a brief sketch of each, as far as he could recall them, and the extent and exactness of his recollection were astonishing. It appeared that when the "Macedonian" was ordered home she was detailed for duty at New York, being considered about the poorest of our ships then in service. Vinton and Ferris's father and a young ensign named Herrick had been sent to the scene of hostilities immediately upon their return, but except these and a few of the older officers there were no changes in the ship's detail of officers until the winter of 1862-1863. Herrick was killed in his first engagement, and Ferris's father within a few months thereafter.

"Can you tell me something more about Ensign Herrick?" Ferris asked, since from what Herndon had said, he seemed the only one whose career might fit the facts he had

gathered from Burton. "Was he fond of society?"

"Oh, yes, very — in his cold-blooded way,"
Herndon answered. "He was not popular with
our mess, although he was there no oftener than
was necessary; for he was eternally tagging
after the petticoats. In this last respect, however, your father was not a bad second, Robert—
a peculiarity that I understand you have not inherited."

Ferris smiled, and Herndon continued: "By-
the-by, that reminds me of a bit of romance
that was gossiped generally aboard ship at that
time. Those of us who had known Vinton
well have always considered it the affair of his
life. Your father and he were inseparable and,
indeed, had been, I believe, from childhood.
Your mother had been dead about a year, and
after her death your father got sea duty, I think
to be near Vinton. During the first few months
of our cruise he was an utter recluse, but finally
Phil managed to drag him out of his retirement,
and during the latter part of our stay at Lisbon he developed into a social devotee. Both
he and Vinton spoke Spanish fluently, and of
course were invited everywhere, and went. To
make a long story short, they both fell in love
with the same girl — at least that was the general supposition — the daughter of an old Eng-

lishman living in Lisbon. Let me see, what was her name?" Herndon stopped for a moment trying vainly to recall it. Ferris tried to appear interested although his thought was of Herrick, who seemed to him the man about whom he must learn more. "The name escapes me just now; I may recall it presently. But no matter," Herndon continued. "Just before we sailed it was commonly rumored, and probably true, that your father and she were engaged and that poor Phil had got the mitten. At any rate from that time he was a very different fellow. Singularly enough, he and your father remained fast friends, but after one experiment the girl's name was never mentioned at the mess when they were present. I have never heard Phil allude to her since, and the matter was soon forgotten when we reached home and found the condition of affairs here. But it has always seemed to account to me for the fact that the old chap has never married."

As soon as might be Ferris again brought the conversation around to Herrick, and before the dinner was over, had obtained from Herndon all the information that the latter possessed regarding him. The evening they spent together at the Club, and when they separated for the night it was with the understanding that they should meet the next morning at the Department in order to verify Herndon's recollection of names and dates.

On his way from the Club to the hotel Ferris walked through La Fayette Square, and in the quiet shadow of one of its dense shrubs, sat down to think over what he had learned from Herndon. To him the most discouraging feature of the case thus far, was the fact that from Herndon's account Herrick (toward whom the circumstances, as he viewed them, pointed most strongly as the subject of his search, on the assumption, at least, that Madge's father was an officer of the American ship stationed at Lisbon) was so flippant and frivolous in affairs of the heart that in all probability he had never married. Herrick's sister was living at their old home in Boston, and Ferris decided that he would visit there, stopping in New York long enough to look up the sailor Vironi and to get Vinton's package from the Surety Company's office. But he anticipated obtaining little information of value from Vironi that could serve him on this side of the water.

When Herndon reached the Navy Department the next morning he found Ferris awaiting him, and within an hour they had consulted the records and found that the information given by Herndon the evening before was in all essential points correct. There was nothing more, therefore, to he done except to institute a search for the letter that Madge's mother had written to the Secretary of the Navy twenty-six years before and for the answer to it. For obvious reasons Ferris had avoided mentioning to Herndon the name of Seaton, or informing him definitely as to the object of his investigation. Now, however, he felt that the secret would be safe with him, and if he were to be of further assistance he must know all. It seemed more than probable to Ferris that Herndon should have known Herrick's friends and might recognize Madge's mother even from the meager description that Burton had given of her.

After Herndon had dispatched the routine work of his office they went to luncheon together, and during the meal Ferris told him of his recent camping experience and of the conditions that stood in the way of his marriage, and gave him as full an account as possible of the wreck of the "Stella," mentioning also the writing by Madge's mother of the letter to the Secretary of the Navy and its answer. Herndon's face wore a troubled look as Ferris finished the narration.

"Robert," he said, with a solemnity of voice and manner quite unusual to him, "You are following a fool's errand. Take my advice and abandon this search, for its result, I believe, can be only failure or worse."

"There are two reasons," Ferris answered, "why I cannot do so until every possible clue has been exhausted. In the first place I do not believe that there would be any hope of my gaining Miss Seaton if my search should fail, and then, too, I have promised her that I would leave no stone unturned. I am not discouraged yet. I hope to prove that Mrs. Seaton was married to Herrick. Do you recall any one that might answer the description of Mrs. Seaton?"

Herndon paused a moment as if undecided what answer to make; then he said:

"Yes, there was an English girl, whose father had been retired from the diplomatic service and was living on a small pension, I believe. I knew her slightly and a charming girl she was. Her mother was doubtless Spanish or Portuguese, for the daughter was very dark and had the warm blood of the South in her veins. Her name was Margery Thorne."

"Did Herrick know her well?" Ferris next asked.

"Yes, all the younger officers did. She was a great favorite."

"Then do you think it improbable that it may appear that he was married to her?"

"Utterly. Herrick was a man of the world — ambitious, discreet and heartless. He was too aspiring socially to permit himself to marry a woman who had nothing to give beyond her personal attractions, and his sense of honor and discretion were more than ample to save his small heart from any embarrassing entanglements. The code of morals of some men is comprehended in the one word 'discretion.' He was essentially of that type. To such, a *mésalliance* were worse than a crime."

"Might he not have been married to her secretly?" Ferris next asked.

"Yes, such a thing was possible, although altogether improbable. I have known of such follies, but Herrick was not the man to commit them."

The conversation next turned to the probability of finding the letter written by Mrs. Seaton to the Secretary of the Navy, and it seemed reasonably certain that, if found, it must give the name of the officer to whom she at least thought herself married.

"I think it exceedingly doubtful if we can find either the letter or its answer, Robert," Herndon said. "At the time it was written the Department was overwhelmed with correspondence, and its clerical force was altogether inadequate and incompetent to handle the mass of work that the first years of the war brought upon it. Then, too, the records of the Department have been moved a number of times from one building to another, and have been ransacked so often and so carelessly, that they are just now in a most unsatisfactory condition. Still, I will make every possible effort in this direction, but it may require much time. I will write to you as soon as the search is concluded. In the meantime what shall you do?"

"I will go to-night to New York and from there to Boston, for I still believe that something may be learned from Herrick's family. Failing to gain any information there, I will return to Chicago and see Vinton and then arrange to go abroad to continue the search."

A half-hour later, Ferris went to the hotel, and having packed his bag, took the four o'clock train for New York. Notwithstanding all that Herndon had told him regarding Herrick, he still believed that the man was Madge's father and that it only remained to establish the fact that her mother and he had been married. This he hoped to learn in some way from Herrick's relatives.

When Ferris left him, Herndon found himself in a quandary. From the description of Mrs. Seaton he believed that she was no other than Margery Thorne, to whom Ferris's father

supposed to be engaged at the time they sailed
from Lisbon. He had not the heart to tell Ferris this, yet when he had gone he regretted that
he had not done so. In the light of what he
had learned he now believed that Edward Ferris
and Margery Thorne had been secretly married
and that for some reason the fact had never
been made public. When they sailed from Lisbon, it was supposed that the rebellion was but
little more than a political scare and that a few
months at most would see it completely crushed
out. Doubtless Edward Ferris felt sure (at least
so Herndon reasoned), that at the end of that
time he could return and claim his bride. But
on reaching this country, the serious condition of
affairs rendered it impossible to obtain a leave
of absence even had he asked for one, and his
death occurred within a year thereafter. Whether
or not it could be proved that there had been a
marriage, Herndon was convinced that Edward
Ferris was Margery Seaton's father. His first
impulse was to follow Ferris to New York and
explain fully to him the miserable situation.
He realized that something should be done, and
without delay. After walking the floor of his
office during the greater part of the afternoon,
he decided that the better (and for him, easier,)
course would be to write to Ferris and to Vinton
also. His letter to Ferris was characteristic of

the writer — brief, straightforward and full of
sympathy. When he had finished it he was tired,
for into his easy-going life such worrisome matters seldom intruded, and the letter to Vinton
was left for the morrow.

When Ferris received Herndon's letter on the
morning after his arrival in New York, he was
incensed, for it seemed to him altogether unreasonable that Herndon, knowing his father as
intimately as he had, could think it possible that
he had acted so dishonorably. Had the letter
set out as fully as Herndon had explained to
himself, how his father had doubtless intended
to return to Lisbon without delay, but how,
under the existing condition of affairs such a return was rendered impossible, it might have had
more weight. As it was, it did not shake his
belief in the correctness of his own view in the
least, and without answering the letter he tossed
it into the fire.

On reaching the office of the Surety Company
he was disappointed to find that Judge Durham
was in Boston and was not expected to return
for several days. Without his order it would be
impossible to obtain the package Vinton had requested him to bring. As there was no train
leaving for Boston until evening, he decided to
find, if possible, the sailor, Vironi. This he
accomplished after a hunt of several hours

through the most villainous part of the city. But Vironi was in such a drunken state that nothing whatever could be learned from him.

When he reached Boston on the following morning, Ferris found Judge Durham, whom he had long known, and obtained from him the necessary order to enable him to get Vinton's package. After this, he looked up the address of Miss Herrick and discovered that she lived but a short distance from his hotel. The house was on the edge of the business centre of the city, and most of its neighbors had already yielded to the inroads of trade. He had not attempted to formulate any plan of questioning Miss Herrick, and as he waited her coming in the old fashioned drawing-room, he began to feel not a little embarrassment. But this disappeared as soon as she entered and learned that he was the son of her brother's classmate. She evidently considered herself as of the navy, because her father had been a commodore, and regarding Ferris in the same light, she received him most cordially. As delicately as possible, he explained to her that he was endeavoring to obtain information in regard to certain of his father's friends, and she, no doubt thinking that he was engaged upon some historical sketch, was profuse enough in her elaboration of her brother's bravery, his intelligence and other

good qualities, real or imagined, that to her
mind might interest the public.

"Was your brother married or engaged to be
married at the time of his death?" Ferris at
length asked, as Miss Herrick had failed thus
far to enlighten him on this one important point.

"I scarcely think that sad affair of his can interest the public, Mr. Ferris," she answered
rather coldly.

"Indeed, I had no thought to make it public,
I assure you. It was merely my interest that
prompted me to ask," said Ferris, now feeling
certain that he was in a way to discover that his
conclusion in regard to Herrick was correct.

Miss Herrick hesitated a moment before answering.

"My brother was to have been married on the
day on which he was killed. When he returned
from Portugal in 1861, my mother and I met
him in New York, since it was impossible for
him to obtain leave of absence. His *fiancée*
was then travelling in Europe with her parents,
but it was arranged that she should be married
from our house. When she arrived she found
that he had been ordered to the South, and within
a week came the news of his death. The poor
girl never recovered from the shock, and two
months afterwards died here. That is her portrait," and Miss Herrick pointed to a painting

of a beautiful young woman — a perfect type of a delicate blonde.

For the first time since he left Madge, Ferris was discouraged. He had felt so confident of success after what he had heard from Herndon, that it was with a feeling of heartsickness that he turned from the Herrick homestead and late in the day took the train for New York.

On the morning after his return he again sought the sailor, Vironi, and finding him comparatively sober, questioned him with particularity as to the last voyage and wreck of the " Stella; " but beyond the fact that Mrs. Seaton had boarded the ship from a small boat, after they had cleared from Lisbon, and that she was given the captain's stateroom and treated as a " great lady," as Vironi expressed it, nothing was learned from him. After this new disappointment Ferris scarcely knew what step to take next. That Mrs. Seaton and Margery Thorne were one, he was confident, but that his father should have married and deserted her he could not believe for a moment.

It was with a heavy heart that he decided to return to Chicago and learn from Vinton what he might recall of her, before attempting to follow the search further, either in this country or abroad.

In the afternoon he went to the Surety Company's office and obtaining the package for Vinton, returned to his room at the hotel. Exhausted by the travel and anxiety he had undergone since leaving the woods, he threw himself upon the lounge, hoping to get some sleep, as his train for Chicago did not start until evening. Vinton's package, which was scarcely larger than a card-case, was tied with a small, faded ribbon. Ferris had put it in the inside pocket of his coat, and when he threw this over the chair, he heard the package drop on the floor. He rose to get it and found that the ribbon had broken and that the small leather case had fallen open upon the floor. As he stooped to pick it up he could not fail to see that the case contained two miniatures on porcelain. One was a portrait of his father and the other a perfect picture of Madge. In a moment it came back to him, how as a little child, Vinton had often shown these to him, though of late years he had not seen them.

Could it be that Herndon was right and that his father had married Margery Thorne? Goaded almost to despair by this thought he restlessly walked the floor of his room, till, with a sudden determination to end his suspense, he hastened to the telegraph office and sent a message to John Brent, requesting him to have Vinton come at once from Round Lake camp to Burton's cabins.

CHAPTER XI.

THE day that Ferris left camp was the unhappiest Madge had ever known. After leaving Burton she walked back over the trail for some distance, but as she neared the camp the thought of being with others seemed unbearable, and she turned into the woods, wandering aimlessly on and on until the deep shadows warned her that it was growing late.

"Coward, coward, that I am," she said half aloud, as she turned to retrace her steps, "to whimper and pine while he hopes and works. Oh, Robert, I am not worthy of your love. Forget me and be happy, dear." She paused as the pain of the thought possessed her. In helpless despair she looked up with her hands clasped across her breast. The glorious coloring of the September sky, the touches of the setting sun upon the tops of the taller trees, caused her to forget the gathering gloom about her, and from the depths of her heart she prayed for courage, for faith and strength. A prayer so fervent as hers, born as it was of infinite yearning for faith and in a heart normally full of courage and strength, could not but bring its own answer, and as it came she said : " Robert, I will wait and hope and pray and love you, always — yes, and I will work, too, and perhaps — perhaps — " but so fast did her heart beat with the new-born hope and resolve, that words failed her, though the color of her cheek and the brightness of her eye told the thought, and she returned to camp as joyous as she had left it miserable. To one of her temperament the pendulum of emotion swings quickly to extremes.

As she passed on to the trail leading to camp she met a woodsman who had been sent in with the mail. Taking it from him she hurried on. Dan'l had just announced dinner, and as the party took their seats she distributed the letters. Mrs. Elting had expected her husband, but was consoled in a measure by a letter that told her his coming would be delayed only a few days. For Helen and Moulton there were several letters, and for Vinton and Whitney an accumulation of daily papers. Moulton glanced hastily at his letters and cramming them into the pocket of his coat, said carelessly, " A choice assortment of bills and club notices." Helen's face brightened as she read the cheerful letter from her mother, and passed it to Whitney. But the color came to her cheek as she opened the next letter, the

handwriting of which she recognized as Mr.
Blake Kennedy's. Moulton, from his seat across
the table, noticed this, and as he could not fail
to see the masculine handwriting, it made him
decidedly uncomfortable. Nor were his suspicions allayed when Helen, in answer to a
question from Whitney, said with some embarrassment, "It is merely a note from Mr.
Kennedy."

"A note, indeed," thought Moulton — "there
are at least a dozen pages."

What a little thing may impair a man's appetite and happiness if he chance to be in love.
Moulton, usually the life of the table, with an
appetite bordering on the voracious, was now
glum and abstracted, although he made spas-
modic attempts to enter into the general conversation.

As they arose from the table, Helen asked if
the man who brought the mail would return to
the town in the morning. Madge found him in
the cook-tent with Dan'l and learned that he
was on his way to a logging camp some five
miles distant, where he would spend the next
day, and return to the town on the day after,
stopping on his way for the mail. As Madge
told Helen this, she added playfully in a half
whisper: "You need not give Mr. Kennedy his
answer to-night, Helen." Moulton caught the

words, and his feelings were expressed by the
vicious way in which he bit off the end of his
cigar, as he sauntered over to the camp-fire,
stood with his back toward it a few moments,
and then walked down to the landing. Mrs.
Elting and Vinton were soon absorbed in the
papers, and Madge, with outspread map by the
light of the camp-fire, explained to Whitney the
location of a marshy lake several miles away on
which good duck-shooting might be had. The
river ran very near to it, and she suggested that
they all make the trip on the morrow, taking
luncheon with them, and returning for a late
dinner. Whitney eagerly assented to this,
although he would have much preferred to go
with Madge alone, for the others knew nothing of
duck-shooting; but, as Madge was sure they
would enjoy the ride on the river and a picnic
in the woods, he prevailed upon Mrs. Elting,
Helen and Vinton to go, and it was agreed that
they should breakfast at six.

As Moulton came up from the landing, he
saw Helen writing in the dining tent. Madge
told him of their plan, for Whitney had already
begun to make his preparations.

"I think," he said, "that you had better not
count me in. I am really no shot, and would
only be in the way. Besides, I am not feeling
very companionable to-night and shall probably

feel less so to-morrow.   No, I will remain here
and keep camp until you return."

"Helen is going, and I am sure she would
want you to go," answered Madge; and there
was an earnestness in her tone that caused
Moulton to hesitate.   "Now, say you will go,"
she added, as Helen came toward him.

"Yes, I will," he said, as he tossed the end of
his cigar into the fire.

It was arranged that Charley should take
Mrs. Elting and Vinton in the largest boat, that
Madge and Helen should take one of the canoes,
and Moulton and Whitney the other.   Charley,
with Dan'l to help him, was sent at once to get
the boats through the shallow outlet of the lake
to the river, in readiness for the early morning
start; and while Helen and Madge prepared the
luncheon in the cook tent, Whitney helped
Moulton to clean his gun and get ready his ammunition.

"You are not going to wear those clothes,
Tom ?" said Whitney, as he noticed Moulton
laying out a heavy dark blue yachting jacket
and trousers.

"Why not?   They are the warmest I have,
and the thermometer is forty now.   It will be
thirty by morning.   Do you want me to wear a
dress suit ? "

"The color could not be worse.   A duck

would see you ten miles off. You must wear something that will harmonize with the browns and grays of the marsh. These wild-fowl are great sticklers for harmony of colors."

"It strikes me that for a novice in duck shooting you are affecting great wisdom."

"I am simply quoting Miss Seaton, and surely she has passed her novitiate."

"Does this brown sweater suit you better?"

"Yes, that is all right, and your brown canvas cap will be much more suitable, if less becoming, than the Tam O'Shanter you have on."

"All right. Have you any suggestions as to the color of my foot-wear? Would you like me to wear brown shoes, also?"

"That would not be a bad idea, if you had them, but mackintosh hip-boots would be better, as you may have to wade after dead birds."

"Well, I have n't them. I will risk wading in my shoes after all the birds I kill."

Having made all arrangements for an early start in the morning, Whitney replenished the wood in the tent stove, and, with Moulton, went out to the camp-fire. The others were busy with their preparations, and joined them for a few minutes only before saying "good-night."

Shortly after five in the morning Charley aroused the camp with the noise of his busy axe, and within an hour all were on the trail to the river. There had been a heavy frost during the night, and on the tall grass in the open places it glistened in the light as the sun peered above the tops of the pines. The ride down the river in the crisp autumn air was exhilarating, and Moulton regained much of his wonted good humor.

For most of the way the river was narrow, and in places the overhanging branches of the trees upon the opposite banks touched above the stream. The growth was mainly pine and hemlock and cedar, with occasional stretches of sumac and alder bushes, and here and there maple and basswood and birch. Such glory of autumn coloring Helen had never seen, or, at least, had never lived in, and that makes all the difference in the world ; and her expressions of delight waked the echoes of the forest as each turn in the winding stream revealed some vista of new beauty. A ride of an hour brought them to the point of the river nearest to the marsh. Mrs. Elting and Vinton decided to go on down stream to the lumber camp six miles below, where they were sure of a hearty welcome and a noon dinner, warm and substantial if not luxurious.

The marsh to which Madge led the way was a mile or so in length, and many years before had been completely under water, but it was now only a long, narrow pond, at its widest point not over a few hundred yards across. About the center of this and at its narrowest part a colony of beavers had at one time built a dam, the remains of which still offered firm footing from the edges of the marsh. As they came in sight of the marsh Madge disclosed her plan of attack upon the ducks. It was that Whitney should occupy a position on the beaver dam on one side of the lake, and Helen and Moulton should take a like position on the opposite side, while she would push through the pond, in a dug-out that Charley had told her was *cachéd* and in good condition. She had brought her paddle from the river, and finding the boat, managed, with Whitney's assistance, to get it into the water. While doing this there was a whirr of wings overhead, and a bunch of mallards dropped into the pond scarcely out of range. This gave promise of good sport, and as the others hastened to their posts Madge cut an armful of hemlock boughs on which to kneel in the boat. After waiting until she felt sure that Helen and Moulton had reached the dam, she pushed off. She had gone scarcely fifty yards when an old drake rose from the rushes with a warning "quack-quack," and swung in low flight over the point where Helen and Moulton were concealed. Madge was at a loss to account for Moulton's not firing, as the shot seemed to her an easy one, and she thought that possibly she had not allowed him time to reach his position; but standing in the canoe, she could see him on the dam with his back toward her, looking after the drake as he joined a flock at the opposite end of the pond.

" Evidently the first bird was too much of a surprise," thought Madge, as she pushed toward the point of the marsh where the flock had disappeared. So quietly did her boat move that she was scarcely twenty yards distant when, with a terrific splashing and quacking, the flock took wing. She had not intended to shoot, but the impulse was irresistible. Instantly her paddle dropped, and, seizing her gun, she brought down two birds and winged a third. The woods rang with a hundred echoes, and from different points of the marsh a dozen flocks arose. As she slipped in new shells she heard Moulton's gun twice in rapid succession, but she could see that each time he had shot behind. Then came two quick shots from Whitney, and three birds from a passing flock were added to their bag. Again Moulton fired, and by great good luck dropped two, and as they fell his yell of triumph woke the echoes of the woods. The same flock passed over Madge, and left one of its number as the result of a very long shot.

As she pushed ahead looking for her crippled bird, she heard a cry for help, and hurrying on, found Moulton nearly waist-deep in mud into which he had plunged in his eagerness to retrieve his birds, while Helen, already over her shoe-tops, was trying vainly to reach him with the dead branch of a tree. On the point opposite, Whitney was swaying to and fro in paroxysms of laughter in which Madge would have been tempted to join had not the tears in Helen's eyes showed how seriously she viewed the situation. By resting his weight upon the bow of the canoe, while Madge in the stern held it with her paddle as steady as possible, Moulton succeeded after much difficulty in extricating himself and reaching the hard ground of the dam.

"I really think that you should have a conservator appointed for me, Miss Seaton," he said, looking disgustedly at the slime trickling from his overalls and oozing from his shoe-tops.

"You shouldn't mind a little thing like this," she answered cheerily. "It is one of the incidents of duck-shooting. I have been in much sorrier plight. We will build a fire in the woods and you can dry off in a little while. Let us go at once, and by lunch time you will be all right again."

As they started for the woods Whitney called out to Moulton to come over and retrieve his birds.

"Listen to that heartless brute," said Helen, thoroughly indignant at her brother's merriment. "I am ashamed of him."

"Let Merrick have his laugh," said Moulton, beginning to realize the absurdity of what he had done. "Perhaps we can devise some method of revenge before the day is over."

While Moulton was building the fire Madge went after the hamper of luncheon ; on her return she found Helen with her feet wrapped snugly in Moulton's top coat, her shoes and stockings drying before the fire, over which Moulton hovered.

"This is a modified Turko-Russian bath, Miss Seaton," he said, as Madge joined them. "From my head to my waist it is hot air and from that down it is steam.   Have you any directions to give about luncheon ?"

"Helen will superintend that ; but I warn you that Mr. Whitney and I shall bring very large appetites about one o'clock," Madge said; yet as she walked back to the marsh she questioned whether either Moulton or Helen would remember the luncheon at all.

The point that Madge had selected as their rendezvous was a little way back from the edge

of the marsh and on the high ground that had
originally been the bank of the lake. The fallen
trunk of a great hemlock against which Moulton
had placed an armful of boughs, made a comfortable back rest and wind-break for Helen, and
she watched him with some amusement as he
moved around the fire in his effort to dry his
nether garments uniformly.

"I am very sorry to have spoiled the morning
for you," Moulton said, as they heard four shots
from the marsh in rapid succession. "Would
you not like to go to the dam again and watch
them shoot?"

"No, I am very comfortable here, or should
be if I were quite sure that you would not catch
cold from your wetting."

"You need have no fear for me. I never
take cold, and now I am simply toasted. Your
shoes and stockings are dry. You might put
them on while I get more wood for the fire."

When he returned a few minutes later, he
found that Helen had moved the boughs nearer
the fire and had spread his top coat upon
them.

"I know you must be tired of standing and I
have made a place for you to lie near the fire.
You will find it very comfortable, and if you
wish to take a nap I will promise not to disturb
you with my chatter. I have a tablet and pencil

in my pocket and can write a letter while you sleep."

"This is very good of you," Moulton said, as he stretched himself before the fire near her, and then added: "I thought you answered your letter last night?"

"I answered one last night; you know I received two."

"You answered Kennedy's last night?"

"Yes."

"And you wish to write to your mother now and tell her of your engagement."

"Can you imagine anything more proper and filial?"

Moulton rose restlessly after a moment's silence, and stood with his back to the fire, in the embers of which Helen was poking with a stick.

"And this is the end of our long friendship," he said, with a solemnity of tone altogether unusual for him, as he turned toward her. "We have known each other since childhood. I remember how, as a great overgrown boy, I thought it my special province to look after you, for you were such a little wisp of a girl in those days. Have you forgotten when your father told us of his election as president of his railroad and that you would move to Chicago, and how we cried together as we said 'good-bye' in the little park beyond the old school-house? I promised that when I grew to be a man, I would .go west to live and be near you again, and we would have such good times together. Your eyes brightened as you listened to all I said I would be for you and do for you, and you laughed through your tears. That was fifteen years ago. Since then I have seen much of the world. I have had many friends, and the best of them have been women, but none have ever taken the place of the little girl who left me that day with a smile on her lips while I ran over to the barn and cried myself to sleep in the hay. I thought I loved you then, but when we met again years after, the little girl I had known and dreamed of was gone and in her place I found a woman crowned with accomplishments and hedged about with conventionalities."

"Yet we were good friends after that?"

"Yes, but your long absence abroad and the many demands of society upon your time when at home left me little chance to renew the old intimacy, even had you wished it, and in time I came to believe that you had cared for me simply in a childlike way, and to think of the old Leamington days only as a beautiful memory. When I saw you at the concert the night before we left Chicago, I seemed to see in your face the same expression I had cherished for

years, and when you asked me to join your party
my heart beat fast with the hope that here in
these woods, away from the world, we might be
happy as we were then."

"And have you been disappointed ?"

"Indeed, no.   I have compassed a life-time
of happiness in these last two weeks.   You have
seemed like the little girl I loved, only infinitely
dearer to me, Helen, and I have dreamed and
hoped and drifted, never thinking that your
heart might have been already given to another.
Last evening, when you read the letter from Mr.
Kennedy, I remembered that you and he had
spent the summer together; and as I saw the
smile that lighted your face as you finished reading, my heart sank within me and I realized that
your love was not for me.   I stood by the lake
for an hour and tried to convince myself that
perhaps I was mistaken, but when I returned to
the camp and found that you had written, I
knew that my dream was over.   Do not think
me weak to tell you of this now.   I want you to
know that I love you, Helen ; that I have loved
you always, although I have not realized it.   I
know you are fond of me in a way, regarding
me, I think, as a good-natured fellow, light-
hearted and companionable and worthy withal of
your friendship. But, Helen, believe me, I could
not be near you and live without your love.   I

should not have talked to you as I have, perhaps.
It can only make you unhappy."

"But it doesn't. Sit down beside me and I
will tell you why."

As Moulton half sat, half knelt, at her side,
he saw the look of perfect happiness in her face
and his heart beat fast with a sudden hope.

"It is because I love you."

For a moment Moulton seemed dazed, then
laying his great hand upon hers and looking her
full in the face he asked :

"Helen, is this true ?"

"Yes, Tom, it is true. Womanish modesty
should prompt me to say that I never realized it
until now, but honesty compels me to admit that I
have loved you ever since I can remember. I loved
you as a child, although I did not recognize the
feeling as such. You were my ideal boy, and as
you grew to manhood, my ideal man. How my
heart thrilled when Merrick used to come home
at vacation and tell me of your college life. Your
victories in the ball games and boating were
mine, and I am sure your occasional failures in
your studies, lazy boy, distressed me more than
they did you. But what it all meant came to
me, Tom, the day of the great boat race. I am
sure the color in my cheeks matched the crimson I wore for you, when I saw you as stroke oar
get into your boat and heard them say that Tom

Moulton would die before he would lose the race. I waved my hand to you as you pulled to the stake boat, and my heart beat fast when you lifted your cap to me in passing. But, oh ! the half hour of suspense after the start when, with Yale a half length ahead, I heard your 'steady, men, steady' drowned by the shouts of the crowd about me. Then, as the boats came in sight again, with you still behind, I heard a miserable little fellow say, 'Moulton has flunked,' and I could have killed him. But you were saving yourself for the finish —"

"And for you, Helen."

"Yes, and when you swept toward the stake boat I could see the great muscles of your arms drive your boat through the water, gaining at each stroke, until Yale was left two lengths behind as you crossed the line and sank forward over your oar, unconscious. My fainting was scarcely noticed in the tumult about us, but when I regained consciousness I knew what it all meant, Tom; and since then I have never questioned my heart."

An hour later, when Madge and Whitney came for luncheon, carrying their birds between them, they found Helen and Moulton absorbed in their happiness and unmindful of the fact that the fire had gone out and that the promised luncheon was unprepared.

In the radiance of Helen's face Madge read the happiness that had come to her, and leaning over she kissed her on the forehead, whispering softly, "I am so glad, dearest." But no such tender thought possessed the hungry Whitney, who looked at them with well affected severity and said:

"Well, you are an energetic couple. Get up, you lazy fellow, and help me build the fire. Helen, your indolence is a positive disgrace to the family."

Moulton rose lazily and went with Whitney after the wood.

"Merrick," he said, as they passed beyond the hearing of the others, "how would you regard me as a prospective brother-in-law?"

"That would depend largely upon whose brother-in-law you proposed to be. Think of a man of your confirmed habits offering himself to an innocent young woman. You drink!"

"That depends on what you offer."

"And you smoke!"

"I draw the line, though, at your cigars."

"And you swear!"

"I will show you in a minute if you don't stop your nonsense. I have proposed to Helen, and she has accepted me. Do you catch the idea now?"

"Yes, I think so. And having committed the irretrievable folly you ask my forgiveness. Suppose I refuse it?"

"Do you want to, Merrick?" There was a touch of almost childish frankness and tenderness in the tone as he spoke, that was irresistible, and Whitney's voice trembled slightly as he answered:

"It is all right, Tom," and then after a moment's pause, he added: "But don't let it interfere with luncheon again."

The most expert *chef* with unlimited viands at his command could not have prepared a meal more delightful to these happy, hungry four young people, than was afforded by the simple contents of their hamper. The afternoon was far gone when Whitney suggested that they spend an hour on the marsh before starting for camp. Scarcely had they reached their positions when a pair of mallards were brought down by Whitney, and eight more were added to their bag before a shot from Vinton's gun gave the signal that he and Mrs. Elting were awaiting them at the river.

The ride up the river to the trail that led to camp meant an hour's hard paddling, and Madge was not a little fatigued when they reached camp and found dinner awaiting them. Perhaps it was the reaction from the excitement of

the day or the contrast of her own unfortunate
condition with the happiness of her friend, or
both, that brought to her a sense of deepest
melancholy.   Charley had built an unusually
large camp-fire and brought hemlock boughs,
which at intervals he piled on, their resinous
needles crackling as they sent myriads of stars
into the leaves above.   Presently he disappeared,
and from the opposite side of the lake a pillar
of flame rose high above the surrounding trees
and lighted the water and the shores.   He had
fired an old birch tree, the ragged bark of which
burned from root to top with a glorious bril-
liancy.   But neither these things nor Moulton's
joyous voice in the songs Madge loved the best
could dispel her gloom, and she was glad when
she could go to her tent and be undisguisedly
miserable.

It was fortunate for her that Burton came on
the morrow, and more fortunate that he could
tell her, as he had convinced himself he truth-
fully might, that he believed there was a chance
of Ferris succeeding, though how small he
thought that chance he had not the heart
to say.   They spent the greater part of the day
together, and when he told her of his plan to
join Ferris in the search, she felt almost as if
success were assured, so great was her confidence
in his ability to accomplish whatever he under-

took in earnest. And so the pendulum of emotion swung to its highest point, nor did it descend until a week later, when the Indian, Joe, appeared with a note saying that Ferris would be unable to come to the camp and requesting Vinton to meet him on the following day at Burton's cabins.

CHAPTER XII.

WHEN Ferris arrived at Keating on the morning of the second day after leaving New York, he stopped at the mine only long enough to get a horse to take him to Burton's cabins. It was but little after noon when he crossed the river. The clatter of his horse's hoofs on the bridge brought a loud "halloa" from Burton and Vinton, who were awaiting him. The latter had come from the camp only half an hour before and had spent the time in looking over the place. He and Burton had conceived a remarkable liking for each other in their brief acquaintance, which gave promise of ripening into a close and lasting friendship.

As Ferris joined them, his face plainly showed the fatigue and anxiety through which he had passed during his absence. Burton understood the cause of this, but Vinton was much alarmed by it and quickly surmised that some sudden and serious malady had seized him.

"Pray do not worry about my health, Uncle Phil," he said, in hope of allaying Vinton's fears for his health. "Physically I am all right, although somewhat travel-worn. I have sent for you to talk over a matter that concerns me deeply, but it has nothing to do with my health. I will tell you all after luncheon."

As soon as the meal was concluded, Burton excused himself on the plea of going to catch a mess of bass for supper in a lake some two miles distant, and left his guests alone together.

As they entered the living room of the cabin, Ferris took from his pocket the package he had brought for Vinton.

"I must tell you, Uncle Phil," he said as he drew an easy chair for Vinton before the open fire, " that by accident I saw the miniatures, and it was to speak of these that I have asked you to come here."

Instantly the color came to Vinton's face, and he sat erect.

" You mean that you wish to speak to me of your father, Robert? "

" Yes, and of the other."

A frown passed over Vinton's features but disappeared as quickly, leaving only a look of deepest sadness, as he said:

" What do you know of her?"

" But little. It is from you that I hope to learn more."

" Why should this interest you? "

" You will understand when you have heard

what I have to say. Since I left you I have been in Washington. I went there to learn of her whose portrait you have. I had heard that she claimed, shortly before her death, which occurred many years ago, to have married an American naval officer, and I promised to discover, if possible, if this was true."

"Was it on my account that you undertook this detective service?" Vinton asked. But Ferris did not notice the sarcasm in his tone.

"I was not aware until after I went East that she had ever known you. My information was very meagre, although from it I was able to gather that if she was married at all, it was in all probability to an officer stationed at Lisbon in the summer of 1861. By merest chance I met Commodore Herndon at the hotel soon after my arrival. I told him of the object of my visit, and from him I learned for the first time of the relations that had existed between you and Margery Thorne."

At the mention of that name Vinton rose nervously from his chair, and walking across the room, looked out of the window.

"Go on," he said, almost fiercely, as Ferris paused a moment.

"I learned also, that my father had known her well and that it was common rumor at the time the 'Macedonian' sailed for home, that they were engaged to be married. In the spring following, a child was born to Margery Thorne."

Vinton turned suddenly and walked towards Ferris, his face now deadly pale.

" Herndon believes that child was my father's. Do you think it true? "

"I know it to be a lie, and I could kill the man that uttered it." He grasped the mantel shelf for support, as he spoke; so intense was his agitation, that for a moment it seemed that his strength would fail him.

"Thank God for those words. I believed it false until the proof seemed conclusive." And rising from his chair Ferris grasped Vinton's hand and held it fast. "You were my father's friend and have taught me to revere his memory. You have stood ever as a father to me, yet my gratitude for all else you have done for me, for all you have been to me, cannot equal that which I feel now. I should have known that he was not the dastard to win a woman and then desert her."

Vinton winced as Ferris spoke, and sinking into a chair, covered his face with his hands and for a moment was silent. His whole frame trembled with suppressed emotion, and Ferris, attributing it to the sad memories he had awakened, said gently:

"I am very sorry, Uncle Phil, that I have distressed you so. When you know what it means for me, you will pardon me, I am sure."

"My God, my God, have I not suffered enough?"

Again there was a silence, broken by Vinton's asking:

"Did Herndon tell of the birth of this child?"

"No, I knew of that before I saw him."

"Who told you?"

"I have seen her."

Instantly Vinton was on his feet and all excitement.

"You have seen her, Robert? When? Where? Is she alive?"

"Yes, she is alive. But when and where I have seen her I must not say."

"Oh! Robert, as you care for me, I beg you tell me where I may find her."

There were tears in Vinton's eyes as he spoke, and Ferris faltered as he answered:

"I cannot—at least not now."

"Be kind to me, pity me, I beseech you. Why not now?"

"Because I love her, and until I have discovered who her father was, I cannot tell you more."

"Then tell me now, for believe me, I am the child's father."

"You? Oh! my God, can it be true?" and

Ferris turned his back on Vinton and leaning upon the mantel, bowed his head in the agony of despair.

"Will you tell me now?" Vinton asked.

Ferris turned upon him, now with hatred in every feature and word as he spoke.

"No. I love her with my whole soul. I promised her that I would prove that she was a legitimate child, if the search took a life-time. You have blasted my life. For God's sake, never let me see you again."

As he spoke, he turned to the table for his hat, but Vinton stood between him and the door.

"Stay, Robert," he said. "I was married to Margery Thorne."

"Is it true? Can you prove it?" But as he looked into Vinton's face, he added: "No, no, I do not mean that, only tell me again that it is true."

"As God is my witness, I swear it is true. Here is the proof, Robert." And taking the leather case from his pocket, he drew from behind the portrait of Margery Thorne, a folded sheet of paper, faded with age, and handed it to Ferris.

"Can you read it?"

"Yes; it is the certificate of your marriage."

"And the witnesses — can you read their names?"

"Yes; one is my father and the other, Dan'l Rafferty. Why, that is our Dan'l ?"

"Yes. Dan'l remembers it well. The chaplain afterwards became a Jesuit priest and is now in the college of Notre Dame."

Ferris took from his pocket the photograph of Madge that Burton had given him and as he handed it to Vinton said :

"Compare this with your miniature, Uncle Phil, and tell me if you discover a resemblance."

"This is Madge. Yes, she is the image of Margery. That is why I asked you to bring me the miniature. It is startling, is it not ?"

"Not when you consider that they were mother and daughter."

"What do you mean, Robert ?"

"That Margery Seaton is your child."

For a moment Vinton stood as one in a trance, with the pictures before him. Then he broke down utterly and Ferris went out, closing the door softly behind him.

Outside the cabin he met Burton, who had returned for his shotgun, having run across a covey of partridges on his way to the lake. Noticing the color in his cheeks and the brightness of his eyes, he said anxiously :

"I am afraid, Robert, that you have been overtaxing your strength. You really should lie down and let me give you something to quiet you."

"You need not give my health another thought," Ferris answered, with a tone of exultation in his voice. "I am tired I confess, but the cause has gone, thank God. Success is a better medicine than any in your pharmacy."

Burton looked at him a moment, as if to determine if already his mind had not begun to show the effects of the strain under which he had labored; but Ferris steadily returned the look, his face aglow with happiness.

"What does this mean, Robert?"

"It means, dear friend, that all you have wished for me has been realized — and more. Come with me and I will tell you."

They walked by a well-worn path to a spring near the river, where, seating themselves on an upturned canoe, Ferris gave Burton an outline of his eastern trip and of his interview with Vinton.

As they rose to return to the cabin Burton took Ferris's arm in his.

"I think, Robert," he said, "that you know how dearly I love Madge, how intimate a part of my life she has become. I have felt that some time she would marry, and so in a way go out of my daily life. I had not thought that there would ever be another to take my place, but her happiness and my loss have come more gently to me than I could have conceived possible. When

I first met Vinton, I was strongly attracted to him. Indeed, I think that no other man has ever won my affection in quite the way he has. There is much in heredity, and doubtless I have found in him many of the traits that have endeared her to me. I do not feel that I shall lose her; I hope I may not."

There was a touch of pathos in his voice as he finished, which impelled Ferris to say quickly :

"You need not fear, her love is great enough for us all. It will bring us nearer together."

As they approached the cabin, Vinton saw them from the window, and came to the door. He had regained his composure and his face was radiant with happiness.

"My friend," he said, taking both of Burton's hands in his, "can I ever pay the debt of gratitude I owe you ?"

"Pray, do not think of that again. I have had my reward already, and there will still be a place in her heart for me, I am sure."

"Yes, and in mine always."

"In the fall of 1860," Vinton continued, after they had entered the cabin, "I was junior lieutenant. I had just finished a three years' cruise on the South Atlantic Squadron and was assigned to the 'Macedonian,' which was ordered to join the Mediterranean Squadron. She was a dilapidated old ship, and when we put in at Lisbon it was found necessary to make extensive repairs, so that the winter was over before they were completed. Soon after our arrival there I met Madge's mother, and loved her from the first. Her father, Edwin Thorne, was an Englishman who had been in the British Navy at one time and afterwards in the diplomatic service, from which he was retired. Late in life he married, against her parent's wishes, a Spanish girl much younger than himself, who lived but a few years thereafter, and Margery was the child of his old age. For some reason he had conceived a strong dislike for Americans in general, and for our naval officers in particular; and this feeling was intensified as the threatenings of our Civil War grew more distinct and the sympathy of England with the South became manifest. Early in the winter I asked Margery to be my wife. She loved me, but realized the hopelessness of gaining her father's consent to our marriage. By chance he discovered our love, and refused to allow me to visit his house. The only one of our officers whom he seemed to regard with any degre of favor was Edward Ferris, my dearest friend, and through his connivance we contrived occasionally to meet.

"Then came the news that war had been declared and that Sumter had fallen, and close upon it followed the orders for our return home.

We were to wait, however, for the 'Saratoga' to join us from Gibraltar. The night after she reached port we celebrated our departure by giving a ball on board our ship. The chaplain of the 'Saratoga,' Harry Munson, had been a school-mate of mine, and his coming inspired me with the idea that Margery and I should be married, if the opportunity should occur.

"I saw Munson the afternoon before the ball, and he consented to perform the ceremony if it could be done secretly. Margery came to the ball. I begged her to consent to the marriage, and with reluctance she yielded. At that time it was believed that the rebellion would be crushed out in a few months at most, when I could return for my bride. We waited until the supper was announced and all had gone below. Ferris, who was officer of the day, took care that the after-deck was clear, and there we were married, with him and our boatswain Dan'l as witnesses.

"On the run from Gibraltar the 'Saratoga' had sprung her shaft, and the repairing of this delayed our departure some days. Fortunately for us, Margery's father had gone to Cintra to spend a few weeks, as he did periodically, with an old surgeon who treated him for the gout, from which he suffered at times severely. In these last days we were together constantly.

When the ship sailed I little thought that I should never see her again."

Vinton paused a moment, overcome with emotion; then, passing his hand across his eyes, he continued:

"When we reached New York I found it impossible to get leave of absence, for we were ordered South at once to the scene of hostilities. Within four months from the time we left Lisbon, our ship had been in as many engagements with the enemy. In the last of these she was totally disabled and abandoned; with a bad wound on my head, I was left as dead, and was so reported. For weeks I lingered between life and death, my mind apparently hopelessly gone.

"When I began to recover, I found myself in a Confederate prison, and nearly five months were spent there before I was exchanged. God only knows the agony I suffered during those months. I wrote to Margery at every opportunity, urging her to bear up bravely until I could come. In all probability, none of my letters reached her, for no answer ever came. When at last I was sent North, wasted with the starvation and exposure of prison life, I was taken with typhoid fever, and three months passed before I was able to travel. Then I got leave of absence and sailed for Lisbon. On arriving there, I found that Edwin Thorne had died during the winter. His house had been sold, their old man-servant had returned to England, and Margery had disappeared two months before. I spent weeks in Lisbon in the hope of finding some clue to her whereabouts; in the end I learned only that a woman answering her description had been seen to go out, with an infant, into the harbor at night, in a small boat, which was discovered the day following empty and adrift. Beyond that my search was fruitless; but it seemed plain to me that my letters had never reached her, and that, believing herself betrayed and deserted, she had sought this way of ending her sorrow. Time and again since then I have returned to Lisbon, hoping against hope that if by any chance she were alive she might return; yet always with the same result — only disappointment.

"When I saw Madge, as I first did the day before we came into camp, her resemblance to her mother startled me. It seemed to me incredible that two people not closely related could be so alike in appearance and manners, but when I learned that she had relatives here, and understood that she was a native of Delaware, I concluded that my imagination probably had much to do with the resemblance I had found."

During the time he had been talking, Vinton had walked restlessly back and forth. Now he stopped, and handing the miniature and Madge's photograph to Burton, sank wearily into a chair near him.

"Are they not much alike, Tom ?" he asked.

"Wonderfully so, and the portrait of the mother is perfect, as I remember her face."

"And did you know her ? Oh ! I am glad of that. Did she ever speak of me ? Did she think me false to her ?" As he spoke, the tears came into his eyes, for with the fatigue of the long walk from camp and the excitement through which he had just passed, the poor man was utterly unnerved.

Ferris rose and laying his hand tenderly on Vinton's shoulder, said to Burton :

"Tell Uncle Phil all you have told me. I am going now to the camp. You and he can follow in the morning. I think it better that I should see Madge first."

"But are you strong enough, Robert, to make the journey to-day? The trail is not an easy one," Burton said anxiously.

"Yes ; Joe and I will go slowly. It is now four o'clock and we should reach there by eight."

Crossing to the other cabin, Ferris found Joe and Adam busily engaged peeling potatoes.

"Joe," he said, "I have good news for Miss Seaton that she ought to know to-night. Can you take me to her ?"

Instantly the Indian was on his feet.

"Yes," he said. "I get you there in three hours."

"And, Adam, will you put up some luncheon for us?"

"Yes, sah, right away." And at once the old negro began to busy himself with this, while Joe made a pack of his "A" tent and the blankets that he had brought from the camp in the morning. Ferris watched the negro as he went about his work.

"You would be sorry to lose Miss Seaton, would you not, Adam?" he said.

Adam looked at Ferris as if to make sure of his meaning.

"You ain't a-going to take her away from us, is you, Mr. Ferris?" he asked anxiously.

"She is to be my wife, Adam."

Adam was silent a moment as he went on with his work.

"I reckon you'll have to take Mister Thomas and old Adam if you take her, sah. We can't git on without her very well. She's been our chile so many years," he said sadly.

"Nothing would please me better than that," Ferris answered with a smile. "Will you come with us?"

"Yes, sah, Mister Thomas and I'll go where-ever she goes, I reckon, if we're wanted. I'm getting purty old, and I ain't as good a cook as some. But I kin larn, Mr. Ferris, I kin larn."

"But what about Miss Burton, Adam? Would you leave her?" Ferris asked.

"No, sah, you'll have to take her too. She can't git on without Miss Madge, neither."

"Then it is settled, Adam, that we shall all live together. I am sure that it will please Miss Seaton and her father, as well."

"But she ain't got no father, Mr. Ferris."

"Oh, yes, she has, Adam; Captain Vinton is her father."

The old man dropped the loaf of bread he was carefully slicing. "For the Lawd's sake, is that true? You ain't foolin' old Adam, is you, sah?" he asked, his eyes wide with amazement.

"No; it is true. We discovered it only to-day."

"For the Lawd's sake," the negro repeated, in astonishment, and after a moment's pause he added: "But ef she had to have a father, I reckon there ain't no one what would please Mister Thomas more'n the Captain, for. Mister Thomas's taken a powerful likin' to him sence he's been here."

And as Ferris took the luncheon and went to join Joe, he left the old negro still shaking his head and exclaiming at intervals, "for the Lawd's sake."

The sun was getting well down below the tops of the taller pines when they took the trail for Round Lake camp, the Indian in advance and going almost at a dog trot. Ferris followed him in silence for awhile, but at last was forced to ask him to slacken the pace, for he was already beginning to feel the effects of the fatigue and strain through which he had passed.

The darkness came quickly upon them, for the sun had set in a cloud, and time and again the Indian looked anxiously at the sky, which was becoming overcast.

"We get storm," he said, as he lighted the lantern he carried in his hand. There was not a breath of wind stirring, and Ferris noticed that the air was warmer than when he rode through the woods in the morning. On they pushed as fast as his strength would permit, the ominous silence of the approaching storm enveloping the woods like a pall. At length the Indian stopped, and throwing down his pack, said : " We stay here till storm go;" and cutting a sapling a few feet above the ground, he bent it down and threw the tent over it to form a shelter. Scarcely had he done this when there was a noise like that of a ponderous railway train in the distance. Louder and more distinct it grew each moment, until the whole forest about them was resonant with the roar of the coming storm. Then the tops of the trees began to bend beneath the mighty sweep of the wind, and great drops of rain drove them under the shelter of the tent. A moment later, the water fell in torrents, and the rush of the wind driving the sheets of rain before it filled the forest with a deafening noise intensified at intervals by a crash of some great pine or hemlock, as it yielded to the fury of the elements. The storm passed as quickly as it had come, leaving only the sound of the falling rain to break the silence of the night.

Joe spread the luncheon and said :

" Better eat, Robert. Bad trail 'tween here and camp."

But Ferris was too exhausted to be hungry. For the first time he realized how severely he had overtaxed his strength.

" I am very tired, Joe," he said wearily, as he rested his head upon the roll of blankets. " Let me lie here a little while and then I can go on, I am sure." In a moment he was fast asleep.

Nearly two hours later, when the rain ceased, Joe shook him. Waking with a start, he looked at his watch.

" How I have slept ! We must hurry if we are to reach camp to-night. It is nine o'clock now."

"Yes, it take over two hours. Can't go through swamp after rain. Must go round."

To avoid the swamp it was necessary to make a detour of nearly two miles; half this distance was through a burnt-over windfall, overgrown with weeds and brier bushes that concealed the charred and rotten trunks lying about in all directions. Over these Ferris stumbled and scrambled, and by the time the trail was reached he could scarcely drag one weary leg after the other.

"Soon see camp now, Robert," the Indian said, encouragingly, as Ferris leaned wearily against a tree. "Put your arm on my shoulder, I take you all right."

Ferris did as he was bidden and together they plodded on, until at last he was aroused somewhat from the stupor of exhaustion by hearing Joe say, "Here we are. You sit by fire and rest."

It was nearly twelve o'clock, and, except for the occasional sputtering of the smouldering camp fire, the stillness of the night was unbroken.

Wrapping a blanket around him Ferris drew a camp chair close to the fire and, after draining the contents of his pocket flask, was soon asleep. The faithful Indian had no intention, however, of allowing him to spend the night there, for the air was damp and chill; so quietly placing a few pieces of wood upon the fire and throwing

a blanket over his own shoulders, he waited for
Ferris to awake. Scarcely had he seated himself when Madge came from her tent and hurried
toward him.

"Is that Mr. Ferris ?   Is he ill ?" she asked,
anxiously, in a low tone.

"Yes, that Robert. He sleep. He very
tired."

"Get more wood for the fire, Joe, please. I
fear he will be cold."

While the Indian went for the wood Madge
drew over Ferris's knees the blanket, which had
slipped down. The movement awoke him.

"All right, Joe, I can go on now," he said,
sleepily.

"Are you ill, Robert, dear," Madge asked
very gently.

Instantly, at the sound of her voice, his eyes
opened wide and for a moment met her anxious
look with a dazed expression.

"Am I dreaming, dearest, or is it really you?"

"Yes, it is I, Robert. Do not get up. You
must be very tired. Oh ! I am so glad that
you have come back. I should have died without you," she said, taking his outstretched hands
and kneeling on the blanket very close to his
chair.

"I have brought good news, dearest. You
will be very happy. I have found your father."

"Found him, Robert ?   Do you mean that he is alive ?"

"Yes, I have seen him.   Uncle Phil knows him well and will tell you all when he comes in the morning.   Is that not enough for to-night, dearest ?"

"Enough, indeed, Robert.   It means everything to me.   It means our happiness."

Drawing her towards him, Ferris kissed her tenderly on the forehead.   As he did so Joe returned unnoticed with the wood.

"Better go to bed, Robert," he said.   "You get cold here."

CHAPTER XIII.

"REALLY, Tom, your lack of perception in affairs of the heart is truly deplorable," said Helen to Moulton, as she slowly paid out the trolling line from the canoe that he was lazily paddling along the edge of the lily-pads and rushes near the shore on the morning after Ferris's return to the camp. The remark was in way of comment on Moulton's expressions of surprise that Madge had preferred to remain in camp this particular morning rather than join them in trolling for bass around the lake.

"Having made this general observation, the correctness of which I do not question, would you mind indicating its special application ? What particular stupidity have I been guilty of now ?" replied Moulton good naturedly.

"Can't you imagine why Miss Seaton would rather stay in camp this morning? To help your imagination I will remind you that last night she was unspeakably miserable; this morning you see her radiantly happy. Incidentally, I may mention that Mr. Ferris came last night and she saw him. Is the adding of two and two together too complex a problem for your mental arithmetic? If not, I think I may now trust you to discover why she preferred remaining in camp to the pleasure of our society."

"Do you mean to say that you think Bob Ferris is in love?"

"Then, why did he return here at this time? Surely, not to see Captain Vinton, for he was with him yesterday. Nor could it have been for the pleasure of camping with us, for he knew that we are to break camp to-morrow."

Moulton puffed away at his pipe a moment in silence, as if trying to circumvent the logic of her conclusions.

"By Jove, Helen, I believe you are right. Bob Ferris in love! Oh! This is too absurd!" and his hearty laugh woke the echoes of the woods.

"Does it really strike you as so very ridiculous, that a man should allow himself to get in that unhappy predicament?"

But Moulton did not notice the coolness of her manner, as he answered: "For Ferris, surely. Of course it is the most natural thing in the world for a fellow like myself who has always been confessedly fond of women."

"Oh, you have been, have you?" she said with a frigidity of tone that was unmistakable.

"Now, Helen, dear, do not misunderstand

me. Do not be annoyed." And Moulton, laying down his paddle, leaned towards her, extending his hand.   At the same instant there
was a violent strain on the trolling line. Quickly
she began to pull it in but found that the hook
had simply fouled in the mass of weeds at the
bottom of the lake.

"See what you have done, careless fellow,"
she said, with pretended annoyance. " I thought
that I had captured at least a muskallonge, and
you have allowed my hook to tangle in the weeds."

"Never mind, dearest, I know a beautiful
spot on the shore of the little bay just ahead,
where we can disentangle it—and any other
snarls due to my thoughtlessness." And during
the next two hours the canoe rested high upon
the beach, the bunch of weeds still clinging to
the hook, while these two light-of-hearts wandered happily through the shadows of the woods.

Soon after they had left camp, Ferris came
from Vinton's tent, in which he had slept. While
he was eating his breakfast, Madge joined him
from the shore.

" Why did you not go with Miss Whitney and
Moulton? " he asked. " I heard them urging
you."

She hesitated a moment and a touch of color
came to her cheek.

"The reason is such a novel one for me that

I feel just a trifle embarrassed to give it," she replied with a smile, but her eyes told him quite as plainly as words, what the reason was.

"It was very good of you. Where are Mrs. Elting and Whitney?"

"Mrs. Elting started sometime ago for one of the lumber camps with Colonel Elting in his buck-board. He came yesterday. Mr. Whitney is off with Charley for the day, for they took luncheon with them."

"Might we not walk over the trail and meet Uncle Phil and Dr. Burton?"

"Yes, if you are not too tired after your hard tramp of yesterday."

"Indeed, I am thoroughly rested and never felt better—nor happier than now."

"Then we will go. But do you think that they will come by the trail and not by the river? Uncle Tom will know that the trail through the marsh will be bad after last evening's storm."

"That is true. It had not occurred to me. No doubt they will come by the river, and we can wait for them at the rapids."

As they walked together over the familiar way, Ferris said:

"You little thought, Madge dear, when we first came up this path together, less than a month ago, what a burden you were bringing into your life."

"No, I did not think of it in quite that way, I confess, Robert," she answered gently. "And yet I felt even then that you had come into my life as no one ever had before. When I was a very little girl, I used to watch the wreckers on the Delaware coast gathering wreckage on the beach after a storm. Whatever they found they claimed as theirs from the fact that they had found it. Perhaps that is why I felt that you were mine from the first."

"And yet you would have given me up?"

"Yes, for your sake my love would have been equal to that sacrifice, even. I wonder if you will ever know what your going away meant to me. You went in hope, but left me in despair. What a mistake is the saying of the Good Book: 'Greater love hath no man than this, that a man lay down his life for his friends.' But that is all past now, Robert, and we must not think of it again. Tell me of him—of my father."

The question came so suddenly that for a moment Ferris was embarrassed for an answer. Madge noticed this, and misunderstanding its meaning, said: "You told me last night that you knew him. Is he such a one as you would be sorry to call 'father?'"

Instantly the answer came irresistibly:

"Madge, dear, he is the purest, the best man I have ever known."

"Surely you will except dear Uncle Phil?"

"No, I cannot except him, dearest, because Uncle Phil—is—your father." As he spoke Ferris took her hands and held them fast. For a moment she trembled with emotion and as she looked earnestly, pleadingly, into his eyes, her own filled with tears.

"Is God, indeed, so good to me?"

"Yes, darling, to us both. Could happiness be greater than this?"

But for answer, Madge leaned her head on his breast, and his strong arms held her tenderly while the tears of joy came fast.

So slowly did they walk along the river bank, stopping now to admire some especially beautiful vista of coloring brought unexpectedly to view by a sudden bend of the stream, or again to select rare tints of brown or gold or crimson from the autumn harvest, that it was noon when they reached the rapids. From this point the view upstream was unbroken for several hundred yards, and here they waited the coming of Burton and Vinton.

Ferris briefly told Madge of his journey east, omitting his own mental suffering and its cause. When he mentioned the miniatures and how closely she resembled her mother, her face was radiant.

"I cannot tell you the happiness it gives me

to know that I look like her.   He loved her so
dearly that I am sure he must love me for her
sake, Robert.   Day before yesterday, when he
went to meet you at Uncle Tom's, he asked me
to walk part way with him.   We had decided to
break camp to-morrow, and it seemed uncertain
whether he would return to us or not.   As we
parted he took both my hands in his.   'Madge'
he said, 'you must let me come to see you sometimes.   Your companionship has been a great
happiness to me in the past month.   I have come
to think of you almost as if you were my own
child;' and his voice was scarcely audible, as he
added with tears in his eyes, 'you are the image
of one whom I have loved always.'   And what
do you think I did, Robert?   I took his dear
face in my hands and kissed him on the forehead."

While they were talking thus, the moments
flying as lovers' moments will, the canoe with
Burton and Vinton appeared at the bend of the
river above the rapids.   Burton was paddling
and Vinton sat near the bow.   Neither saw Madge
and Ferris.

"Hold on, Tom," said Vinton, cheerily, as
they neared the swift water, "I am too valuable
a cargo for you to risk in the rapids."

"Shame on you, Philip," replied Burton, with
a laugh, as he turned the boat to the shore.
"And you an old sailor, too.   However, the

walk to camp is a short one and will give us a
chance to straighten out. We should not have
needed it twenty years ago."

"Let us help these two elderly gentlemen"
said Ferris to Madge, loud enough to be heard
by them as the canoe touched the shore almost
at their feet.

Madge held the boat while Ferris assisted
first Vinton and then Burton, for both were somewhat stiff after the long ride ; then lifting the
bow upon the shore she turned to Vinton. Once
again she kissed him—this time on the lips. Was
it this or the whispered "father" that brought
the tears to his eyes, as he held her fast in his
arms and bowing his head close to hers, sobbed:
"Margery, Margery — at last, my love."

Madge's face was pale as she gave both hands
and an affectionate kiss to Burton, while Vinton,
by a vigorous use of his handkerchief, endeavored to demonstrate that he was merely troubled
with a sudden influenza.

"Dear Uncle Tom," she said, "I shall love
you only the more for all that has come to me."

Burton was of sterner stuff than Vinton, but
his voice quavered, as he answered : "Yes, child,
you must keep a place for me."

Ferris and he, leaving Madge and Vinton to
follow, went on to camp where they found Helen
and Moulton at luncheon. As Moulton caught

sight of Ferris, he rushed to meet him and even the cautionary "remember, Tom," from Helen, could not prevent his exclaiming: "Bob, you old humbug, I congratulate you, I may also say that I sympathize with you for I —"

"Mr. Moulton!" called Helen sharply, with affected severity.

"All right, Helen, I forgot that I was not to announce our engagement. But pray do it quickly, for I cannot keep the secret any longer. The mental strain is really too great."

"I can't see that you have left anything for me to announce," replied Helen, coloring, as she gave her hand warmly to Ferris and Burton. "I hope that I may congratulate you, also Mr. Ferris."

"Indeed you can, Miss Whitney, for I feel that I am a most fortunate fellow."

During luncheon Helen and Moulton were told of the newly discovered relationship between Madge and Vinton. An hour later when Moulton was urging Helen to go for a last ride on the lake, for Burton and Ferris had strolled off together, she put an end to all argument by saying:

"No, go without me. I must wait for Madge — I am simply dying to get my arms about the dear girl's neck. You are a man and of course don't understand such things."

"Well, don't I?   With half an opportunity, Helen dearest, I think I could convince you of the contrary."

"Tom Moulton, you are simply horrid," she answered, blushing deeply.   "Now go, or I shall not speak to you again to-day."

Some time after, when he returned to camp, he found Madge and Helen sitting together in a hammock with one shawl around them both and with heads very close together.   Helen was right.   Only a woman could comprehend their feelings.

Shortly before dinner Colonel and Mrs. Elting drove into camp, and the little woman's delight at the confidences with which Helen and Madge flooded her was simply boundless.   The Colonel took matters more philosophically.

"I have been urging Dora," he said, "for years, to come into the woods.   There is no such place for romance, even for an old couple like ourselves.   I am sure I have not driven with my arm around her waist in twenty years before!"

"But you know, George, the road was very rough," she replied, apologetically.

"And was that why you kissed me just before we reached camp?   Come, now, admit that it was the woods!"

But for answer she only shook her head in mock severity.

The dinner was delayed somewhat, to await the arrival of Whitney, whose triumphant yell from across the lake announced that his day's hunt had not been without success, and a few minutes later he appeared, bearing upon his shoulders (a burden too precious for the Indian to carry) the skin of the long-coveted bear.

No happier party ever met beneath spreading pine and hemlock than that gathered at this last dinner at Round Lake Camp. Even old Dan'l had caught the spirit of gladness, and gave evidence of the fact by the elaborateness of his *menu*, while Charley and Joe made such a camp-fire as cast in shadow all their previous efforts in this direction. Around this the early part of the evening was passed in much the same way as most evenings are in camp — a sameness that to the lover of camp life is never monotonous. Later, Vinton and Colonel Elting discovered that they both had taken part in the siege of Vicksburg, and their war experiences claimed attention for a while. Then Moulton tuned his banjo and sang some negro melodies in a dialect that Burton assured him would have done credit to old Adam. When he had finished, Madge asked Vinton to sing the old Spanish boat song he had given them once before.

" I can not tell you how that simple old

song affects me.   It seems like an echo of music that I knew long ago," she said gently to him.

"I am glad you like it, Madge," he answered. "It was your mother's favorite song."

As he finished, he saw old Dan'l listening in the shadow beyond the fire.

"Come here, Dan'l," he called, "I wish to speak to you!"

And as Dan'l came nearer, smoothing out his apron, which he had knotted about his waist, he added : "Dan'l, did you ever see any one who looked like Miss Madge?"

Dan'l hesitated a moment, as if in doubt whether Vinton wished him to speak the truth or not ; and he would have done either with equal readiness for him.

"Come, speak out, Dan'l, and mind that you tell the truth."

"Yes, sor ; one lady, sor, if me old eyes serve me."

"Where was it, Dan'l?"

"It was in Lisbon harbor, sor, some twenty-six years ago, when I was boatswain of the 'Macedonian.'"

"Well, go on ; tell all you remember about her."

"Shall I speak of the night of the grand ball, sor?"

"Yes, everything, Dan'l.   You have kept

my secret well; but it shall be a secret no longer."

"Well, sor, if I must, I must. The young lady, whose speaking image sits beside ye, came on the after-deck with yerself and Liftenant Ferris and the parson from the 'Saratoga;' and the parson read from his church book and then called ye man and wife. And the young lady kissed ye and the parson and Liftenant Ferris, and gave me a bracelet she wore on her arm, and I have it yet. That's all, sor, saving the week's jugging I got fer leaving me post midships without notice."

"Miss Madge is the lady's daughter, Dan'l, and my child."

"God help me, Captain! Ye don't mean it, sor," and the old fellow forgetting his embarrassment, came very close to Madge.

"This be the happiest day of me life, Miss," he continued. "I have been hoping since I set eyes on ye that the Captain might win ye for his bride, for it's a poor house we have, Miss, with no women folks at all. What an old fool I be, to be sure. But we'll have ye now anyway, so we will."

"You will have to ask Mr. Ferris about that, Dan'l. They are engaged to be married," Vinton answered, with a smile.

"O my! O my! And ye're engaged at

last, Master Robert. Sure, I never suspected ye of it and ye've not been keeping company at all. Well, Miss," he continued, turning again to Madge, "ye have the foinest father and best husband in the world, so ye have." And Dan'l went back to the cook's tent, and for an hour after was heard humming that sweet old Irish melody, "The Low-back Car."

     *   *   *   *   *   *

Breaking camp is always a dismal affair, but in this case Colonel Elting had robbed it of one most dismal feature, by arranging that the tents should be left standing until after the party had gone, when his men from the nearest lumber camp would pack and send them to the town. At Ferris' request Madge and Vinton decided that they would return with him by way of Keating, spending one night at Burton's cabins. The Eltings, with Helen and Moulton, drove away soon after breakfast. Whitney, with unsated fondness for sport, had gone ahead with his shot-gun some time before in the hope of finding a few partridges basking in the morning sun along the road. From his seat beside Helen the incorrigible Moulton called to Ferris as they drove off : " I shall see you at the Club day after to-morrow, Bob, and arrange for your services as best man, if I can wait so long ! "

"You had better remember the old adage, sir, 'Don't crow until you are out of the woods,'" said Helen.

"I shall not," he answered, and in a lower tone added: "I have been out of the woods, dear, ever since you told me —" but as she raised her finger warningly, he left the sentence unfinished. And taking Moulton at his word, we may safely leave these happy lovers, in the assurance that the world, which loves a lover, will give them of its best.

An hour later Vinton and Burton, with the Indians and Dan'l, started for the cabins, leaving Madge and Ferris to follow and meet them at luncheon beyond the swamp.

The walk to the cabins with Madge was for Ferris a joyous contrast to his last journey over the trail, and when they gathered that evening in Burton's room, he felt that life could offer him no greater happiness than the present.

The start for Keating was not made until after luncheon the next day, as Joe had gone early in the morning to get horses for Vinton, Madge and Dan'l, and to notify John Brent of their coming. As they neared the town Ferris checked his horse a moment, and, looking back down the long vista of pines through which the old logging road ran, said with a half sigh :

"I am sorry, Madge dear, to leave the woods. They have given me happiness beyond any I ever dreamed of."

"I have loved them always, Robert; but never so much as now. We will come again, will we not?"

"Yes, we will come together. They would never be the same without you, Madge."

"If Moulton could only have heard that speech," thought Ferris, "how he would have jeered at me."

At Keating they found that Brent had arranged for sleepers on the night express and that Mrs. Brent had prepared a delicious supper for them.

They had finished this, and the men, with the exception of Brent, who had excused himself on the ground of business, were smoking before the open fire, when there occurred the last incident that need be recorded in these pages. Madge was standing at the window looking down the long road that stretched away to the town, absorbed in watching a great number of lights that, after flickering to and fro like will-o-the wisps, began at last to move in a body toward the mine. "These are the men that come to work in the mine at night," she thought, until the low rumble of voices peculiar to an approaching rabble, reached her ear. Ferris also

heard it, although less distinctly, and asked:
" What is that noise, Madge ?"

" A large number of men are coming this
way, Robert, with lanterns and torches. Do they
always make such noise when they go to work ?"

Instantly he was at her side. Scarcely five
hundred yards from where they stood and moving rapidly toward them, was a vast crowd of
people with lanterns and torches of pine knots,
which they flourished above their heads as they
hurried on.

Turning to Ferris, Madge was struck by his
pallor.

" What does this mean, Robert ? Surely
there is nothing wrong ?" she asked anxiously.

" I trust not, dear. But pray go into the
back room. I shall know in a few minutes."

" And leave you ? Never, Robert."

" And this is their revenge," thought Ferris,
although he did not speak it for fear of alarming
Madge. Burton and Vinton now joined them
and they stood a moment in silence.

" Have we any weapons, Tom ?" Ferris asked
quickly.

Burton paused an instant and then answered
with a smile:

" You are armed sufficiently for this crowd.
You have a good pair of lungs and a reasonably
strong voice. That is all they need. Don't you

see the women and children, Robert, and can't you imagine why they are coming?"

In a moment the meaning of it all flashed upon Ferris and he blushed crimson. The crowd now gathered about the broad veranda and the voices were hushed. A little fellow with cap in hand was pushed forward and timidly came up the steps. It was Willie, the mail boy, and he said that the men would like to see Mr. Ferris before he took the train.

"Go out and give them a speech, Robert; that is what they want," said Burton, pushing Ferris toward the door.

"But what can I say?"

"Oh, anything will please them. You need not be eloquent."

What he did say (although he never could remember) must have pleased them, for he was constantly interrupted by applause and cries of "Hear, Hear" and "Good" in a dozen different languages.

As he finished, an old Scotch woman with a shawl about her kindly work-worn face, asked: "Mayn't we see yir lady, sir? We'ill luve her for the maister's sake."

Ferris turned, and Madge came quickly to his side.

"And I will love you all, good people, because you love him."